Rainbows over O'Mara's

Book 12, The Guesthouse on the Green

Michelle Vernal

In memory of Kitty Robson, my Scottish friend and her lovely daughter, Diane. I shall miss our banter x

Chapter One

♥

Dublin, December 2001

'Quinn, could you not read something interesting?' Aisling gestured to the copy of Gina Ford's *The Contented Little Baby Book* resting on the coffee table before nibbling on her gingernut biscuit. *Morning* sickness was a fallacy because she felt sick morning, noon and night and had done for the last four weeks. 'I didn't enjoy learning the times tables the first time around, and I'm not enjoying them now,' she snapped. 'And, you're driving me mad with the "ABC Song". Sure the jelly bean's only just reached the three-month mark. So, singing the song and reciting the times tables isn't going to ensure him or her a place at Trinity.'

'Aisling, I'm setting our child up for a bright future. A parent always wants their child to do better than they did.'

'Just because you were considered disruptive and spent a great deal of your primary school years with your nose pressed to the classroom window on the outside looking in doesn't mean the jelly bean will.' Aisling brushed biscuit crumbs off the sweater she'd chosen to wear to the ultrasound appointment that morning. It was sage-coloured, bringing out the green in her eyes and red glints in her hair. She wanted to look her best when she saw her baby for the first time.

At the moment, she needed all the help she could get too. Dark circles had taken up permanent residence under her eyes even though she'd slept heavier than she'd ever slept for the last couple of months. It didn't seem to matter whether she got eight hours or not because she was knackered all the time. Her hair was lank too, despite using the salon-only Wella Balsam shampoo she'd splurged on.

Meanwhile, Moira's hair looked suspiciously shiny and full of bounce. Aisling was thinking about marking the bottles.

According to her pregnancy guide, the sickness plaguing her would ease once she hit twelve weeks. But so far, there was no sign of it letting up.

Aisling wanted to shout about the jelly bean from the hill-tops or at least be able to share their happy news, but after the initial excitement of realising they were pregnant, she and Quinn had erred on the side of caution. They'd decided not to broadcast that they were going to be parents until they'd reached the magical three-month marker and had their first scan. Only their nearest and dearest, including her best friend Leila, Ita, and an Austrian guest who'd been in reception when Aisling had flown down the stairs of the guesthouse waving a pregnancy test stick with two pink lines knew.

Poor Mammy was fit to burst with having kept quiet this long. They all were, for that matter.

The days between that initial euphoria of a positive test to reaching the twelve-week point had dragged. Finally, however, Aisling could relax into her pregnancy. In contrast, Quinn had been confident that everything would be alright from the get-go embracing impending fatherhood to the point of being annoying. Very annoying, she thought, tuning in to what he was saying.

'I know, Aisling, but reading aloud about sleeping and feeding routines won't benefit him or her. Unlike the alphabet and the times tables. It's a dog-eat-dog world out there, and I'm trying to give our child a head start.' He got up from the sofa where they were sitting like Tweedledee and Tweedledum, waiting until it was time to leave, and smoothed imaginary creases from his jeans before sitting back down again.

Quinn had been antsy all morning, as had Aisling, who was beginning to think it would have been better if he'd gone to the bistro for a couple of hours. Her bladder was fit to burst, and she crossed and uncrossed her legs to take her mind off it. They were feeding off each other's edginess.

'It will so be beneficial. The jelly bean will know what's expected of him or her as a newborn.' She didn't believe this for one second not having borne witness to Kiera's first months in the world. But she lived in hope as all new mammies did that she would be the one to set her baby's routine, not the other way round. 'Besides, babies in the womb can pick up on their mammy's stress, so they can, and the ABC song is making me stressed.' Aisling craned her neck, trying to see the time on the microwave in the kitchen. *Surely it must be time to go.*

'It's ten thirty,' Quinn informed her. 'We'll leave in fifteen minutes. Do you think you have room for one more glass of water?'

'No!'

'It's just you're to have a full bladder for the ultrasound.'

'I'm aware of that,' Aisling said through gritted teeth. She was also aware she was being short with her husband. 'Sorry. I know I'm being awful, and you're trying to be helpful, but you're being—'

'Annoying?' Quinn grinned.

Aisling nodded, her fractiousness disappearing at the sight of his smile.

A cell phone ringing saw them both reaching for their mobiles. Aisling's was in her bag, Quinn's in his pocket.

It was Aisling's.

'Mammy,' she said, rolling her eyes at Quinn. She'd be ringing to give wheedling her way into the scan with them one last shot.

'You don't have to answer it. Ring Maureen back after the appointment, then you can tell her how it went.'

'This is my mammy we're talking about.'

The ringing seemed to grow more impatient.

'You're right.' Quinn got up.

'If you're going to the toilet, do NOT wee loudly.'

Quinn saluted her and Aisling took a deep breath and answered her phone. 'How're you, Mammy?'

'As well as to be expected given my exclusion.'

Aisling sighed. 'I've explained it to you, Mammy. Quinn and I want it to be just the two of us when we see our jelly bean for the first time. Maeve understood.'

'Maeve Moran didn't give birth to you, now did she?'

'If she had, it wouldn't bode well for Quinn and I's relationship.'

'Don't be smart, Aisling O'Mara.'

'O'Mara-Moran.'

'Rosemary Farrell says it's the maternal nana's right to attend all the appointments. She went to all of Fenella's.'

Aisling thought that Rosemary Farrell could jam her hiking pole somewhere the sun didn't shine. It was time for a change of tack, she decided. Diversion was the best way to deal with Mammy when she'd a bee in her bonnet. 'Sure, and how is Rosemary? You're back on speaking terms, I take it.'

There was a sniff at the other end. 'She's not a gracious loser,' Maureen began.

And you're not a gracious winner, Aisling thought but kept this to herself. Mammy had taken gold home in the Howth Quilters Association's Memories section and behaved as though she'd won Ireland's Person of the Year Award.

'But Cathal Carrick, the cobbler, you know, her new man friend who made her the special boots that have her bounding around the Howth hills like the bionic woman?'

Aisling tried to keep up. She'd a vague memory of a man who'd been wrapped around Rosemary at Mammy and Donal's housewarming. He'd brought Chinky, Peter and Molly's pixie friend from her beloved childhood, Enid Blyton Wishing Chair series, to mind. 'Yes.'

'Well, he set the pair of us up, so he did. First, he lured me into visiting his cobbler's shop, promising to make me some special boots like Rosemary's. Then he lured Rosemary into the shop,' Maureen hesitated. 'I'm not sure under what premise, but I have my suspicions because there was no one to be seen when I arrived at the shop, but I could hear certain noises, and they emerged from out the back looking hot and bothered when I rang the bell.'

Aisling groaned. 'Don't, Mammy. I feel sick as it is.'

'You young people are all the same. You think you invited the bedroom shenanigans so.'

This conversation was veering into dangerous territory, Aisling thought, getting her mammy back on track. 'You said Cathal the Cobbler lured you and Rosemary to the shop, and then what?'

'It was all very awkward, but then I decided to be the bigger woman, and I told Rosemary her memory quilt was very good and that it must have been a tough decision on the judges' part.'

'And that did the trick?'

'No, it did not because Rosemary implied I'd attempted to bribe the judges by offering them free pairs of Mo-pants.'

'Did you?' Aisling wouldn't put it past her mammy.

'I did no such thing. Sure, I'm a businesswoman, Aisling. You don't get rich giving your stock away. I merely offered them a generous discount, and it was only good manners on my part to say thank you for giving up their time to judge the competition in the first place. There was no attempted bribery. I told Rosemary she was being slanderous suggesting such a thing and walked out, so I did.' Maureen bristled with self-righteous indignation.

Aisling sensed there was a 'but then' coming.

'But then, Cathal came running after me offering a fifty per cent discount on the special boots I was after if I'd share the gold ribbon with Rosemary on a month about basis.'

'A bribe.'

'It wasn't a bribe, Aisling. It was a tempting offer because my knees have been aching lately. The long and short of it is I went back into the shop and conceded the competition should have been a tie and could we not share the ribbon and let bygones be bygones.'

'And after all that, do you have your special boots, Mammy?'

'Not yet. Cathal's after telephoning earlier to say he'll have them finished for me next week. Kiera, don't be putting that in your mouth!' There was a clatter as the phone was dropped, and a wail went up a second later. At nine months old, she was a demon for putting things in her mouth, a problem exacerbated by her latest trick, crawling.

Maureen came back on the phone. 'She was after trying to gnaw on Donal's flip-flop again.'

'Jaysus wept, Mammy! It could still have the fungal toe germs on it! Why's his flip-flop in the living room anyway. It's only three weeks until Christmas. Sure, his toe would fall off if he ventured out in them in this weather.' Thus far, December was bleak, and Aisling's eyes flitted to the window and the outside downpour.

'It's Pooh's fault, so it is. He's gone from being resentful of Donal's presence to hero-worship, and he can't bear to be parted from him. The flip-flop to Pooh is what blankie was to Patrick. It was a manky thing that blankie, but your brother dragged it everywhere, refusing to be parted from it. Pooh's the same because I no sooner tuck the flip-flops away in the wardrobe than he carts them out again.'

'Throw them out, for feck's sake!'

'Aisling O'Mara, the jelly bean will hear you. Wash your mouth out.'

'O'Mara-Moran.' Aisling corrected her for the second time.

Maureen ignored her. 'How're you feeling this morning?'

'Well, I'm bursting to go to the toilet. The information sheet from the clinic said I'm to have a full bladder for the ultrasound. I'm terrified I'll have an accident before we even get out the door!"

'Ah, sure now, cross your legs on the way there, don't run any taps, and you'll be grand. How's the sickness this morning?'

'The same. I've had my head down the toilet twice already. It's not fair, Mam. Rosi and Moira didn't have a day's sickness between them when they were pregnant with Noah and Kiera. And don't you dare sing me the "Soldier-On" song!'

'I wouldn't dream of it, and fair doesn't come into it, Aisling. They've strong constitutions, those two. Like oxen the pair of them. You were always the one who got the flu instead of just a cold. And you know I was terrible sick with you but not with Patrick or your sisters. I sailed through those pregnancies, although the childbirth was another matter with your pumpkin heads.'

'Mammy, stop with the pumpkin heads. I don't want to think about that yet. And what's your point anyway?'

Maureen had forgotten her point and then, realising she didn't have one said, 'I thought you'd be the awkward child as a result of all the sickness, but no, it was Moira who gave me the headaches.'

Aisling frowned. 'So are you saying I'm going to have an easy baby?'

'Not necessarily, but you'll love him or her something fierce either way. Aisling, I've got to get the babby. Kiera's going for the Christmas tree! You're to tell the santana person to take a nice, clear photograph of my grandchild and ring me as soon as you've had the scan, do you hear me.'

'It's sonographer, Mammy, and I hear you.' But the line had already gone dead.

'Ash, are you ready to go?' Quinn reappeared in his jacket.

One thing about Mammy, Aisling thought as he helped her into her jacket; she was a great distraction. Then, tossing her phone in her handbag, she followed her husband out of the door.

Chapter Two

♥

Aisling and Quinn paused briefly on the second-floor landing to say good morning to Mr and Mrs Jones from Wales. Mr Jones, an affable man with a generous girth, was patting his pockets down for the room key and produced it triumphantly as Mrs Jones replied to Aisling's enquiry about how their breakfast had been in an indecipherable Welsh brogue. Aisling smiled and nodded even though the dark-haired woman could have said it was awful, for all she knew.

Ita had her head in the cleaning cupboard at the end of the hall on the first-floor landing when they reached it, and upon hearing her humming happily, Quinn looked back over his shoulder at his wife with raised eyebrows.

Aisling shrugged. Miracles never ceased, and she preferred this loved-up version of their director of housekeeping to the Idle Ita of old. This new and improved Ita had the bathrooms sparkling, and she tucked sheet corners into the beds with hospital-sharp precision. As for the banister rail, she was currently resting her hand on, it gleamed. Yes, finding a fella had done wonders for Ita's work ethic.

Bronagh was on the telephone, and Aisling's practised eye did a sweep of the reception area as she ticked off her mental checklist. The cushions on the sofa were plumped, magazines arranged neatly on the side table, the brochures advertising the delights of Dublin and beyond well stocked, and the pink peonies in the arrangement of fresh flowers on top of the reception desk were giving off their sweet fragrance. She nodded to herself approvingly. Good. Everything was ship-shape. They couldn't afford for there to be anything amiss.

'One sec,' Aisling said, holding up her index finger to Quinn, who was already at the door as she waited for Bronagh to finish her call.

'I'll bring the car around,' Quinn said, not waiting for a reply and, opening the door pulled the hood of his jacket on.

'We'll look forward to seeing you on the twelfth of January, Mrs Simmons. You be sure to have a lovely Christmas now. Thank you, I will. Goodbye.' Bronagh smiled into the receiver, and as she put the phone down, Aisling's mobile rang.

'Feck off,' Aisling mumbled, digging it out and, seeing it was Mammy again, she ignored it. 'Morning, Bronagh. How's your mammy doing?' she asked overtop of the insistent ringing. Mrs Hanrahan had struggled with her health for years but had been especially poorly in recent weeks.

Aisling was putting Bronagh's absentmindedness at work these last months down to the strain of her mam's illness. She'd forgotten to pass on guest messages, and double bookings had been made. All of which was out of character. Luckily, Freya, their night receptionist, had sorted the issues out, and Aisling hoped Bronagh would be back in top form after a decent break over Christmas.

Because of her upcoming holiday, Aisling hadn't mentioned these slip-ups to Bronagh. But, if they continued in the new year, she'd have to broach them. What if something was wrong with her? Aisling's mind raced ahead, imagining worst-case scenarios, but she shut those thoughts down. She was getting way too far ahead of herself.

'She seemed brighter this morning, thanks, Aisling. Knowing Lennie will be over soon is a tonic for her.'

'And for you.' Aisling smiled. She was very fond of their receptionist, who was like a second mother to her at times. A warm glow settled over her, thinking of Bronagh and their long-time guest, Leonard Walsh's romance. She'd had a part to play in it, after all.

'And for me,' Bronagh agreed. 'I'm looking forward to a few weeks off, and sure, it was grand Freya offering to step in and cover my shifts for the fortnight. I know it was a juggle for her with college re-opening the second week I'm away. But I'll be able to relax now, knowing O'Mara's is in safe hands and that you won't be overdoing it.'

Bronagh was waiting for her to reply, and Aisling summoned a bright smile. 'You deserve a decent break with plenty of R & R, and you're right too. It did work out well.'

Bronagh asking for time off was usually the stuff of night-mares, but Aisling didn't begrudge her it in the least. The problem was that in O'Mara's trusty receptionist's absence, it usually fell on her to fill in on the front desk on top of her usual management tasks. So by the time Bronagh returned, she'd been run ragged and needed a holiday.

There was no way she'd have managed it this time feeling so rundown, and she'd nearly kissed Freya when she'd suggested she cover the eight am until four pm shifts. James and Evie, the part-timers who worked on the weekends, were eager to boost their student income by divvying up Freya's usual Monday to Friday evening hours. As such, everything had fallen into place nicely.

'How's Joan getting on these days?' Aisling asked in a change of subject. Joan Walsh was Leonard's sister, and while Leonard had long ago crossed the water to Liverpool, she'd remained in the family home in Dublin.

'Would you believe she's invited Gordon, Lenny, myself and Mam to the house for our Christmas dinner?'

'Ah, that's wonderful, Bronagh.' Joan's life had not been easy, but things began to change for the better when Bronagh came on the scene.

Aisling remembered what else she'd wanted to ask Bronagh. 'Did the Bridsons get away alright on their Avoca Valley tour this morning?' It was a terrible day for sightseeing, but at least they'd enjoy the pub lunch at Fitzgerald's. The food was always good and the atmosphere cosy and convivial.

'They did, or at least I think it was them. I could barely make their faces out under their rain ponchos. Sure, it's lovely weather for ducks, so it is, and by my reckoning, they should be trying to spot the Guinness Lake through the deluge out there as we speak.' Bronagh gave Aisling the once-over, her eyes fastening on the sweater beneath her jacket. 'That colour looks very well on you.'

'Thanks, Bronagh. Your hair looks nice.' Aisling repaid the compliment noticing the white stripe down her parting was gone. Bronagh sat up straighter in her seat, fluffing her Cleopatra-esque hair.

Aisling pictured another of their guests with hair just as dark as Bronagh's, Sara Scott and was almost afraid to ask after her, especially given Bronagh's recent blunders.

The young woman from Belfast had arrived the day before, and Bronagh had inadvertently caught their latest arrival taking photos of the guest lounge. The lounge, with its high Georgian ceiling, carefully chosen furnishings and large sash windows through which colourful flower boxes on the sills partially hid the street beyond, was a photogenic room. So, taking photographs of the room wasn't unusual. What was strange, however, was how Ms Scott had rifled through the selection of beverage sachets as though inspecting them.

Bronagh had continued to watch, perturbed, from the doorway as Ms Scott, unaware of her presence, trailed a finger across the buffet before inspecting it for dust. Then she'd gone on to check the dates on the pile of glossy magazines on a monthly subscription for their guests' reading pleasure.

Bronagh relayed this odd behaviour to Aisling, who'd been sure to keep a watchful eye on their Northern Irish guest the day before. Little things hadn't sat right with her, and her keen eyes had picked up on how Ms Scott had held her cutlery up to the light at breakfast, scrutinising it. Most tellingly of all, though was, given she'd purported to be in Dublin to attend a three-day sales conference, she'd barely left the guesthouse all day. It didn't add up, and Aisling had worked in the hospitality industry long enough to know when something wasn't right. She smelled a rat.

The thing was, Sara Scott was a nondescript woman. She favoured comfortable, if not a little frumpy sweater and trouser combos, wore minimal makeup, and had sharp eyes that missed nothing behind the lens of her glasses. Her dark hair sat squarely on her shoulders and was held back with an Alice band. She reminded Aisling of a mouse. There was nothing about her to make her stand out from the crowd. You'd barely notice she was there. All attributes, Aisling knew, stood an undercover hotel inspector in good stead.

She relayed her suspicions to the O'Mara's staff with instructions that they were to bend over backwards where Ms Scott was concerned.

'Was everything to Ms Scott's satisfaction at breakfast this morning?' She steeled herself for the response.

'Mrs Flaherty told me she sent her breakfast back to the kitchen claiming her egg was too runny given she'd asked for her eggs over easy.'

Aisling bit her bottom lip, feeling a spike of anxiety. Of all the employees Sara Scott could test, she'd had to pick Mrs Flaherty. Aisling knew O'Mara's breakfast cook did not take well to criticism where her full Irish was concerned. The customer was not always right, in Mrs Flaherty's opinion.

'You'll be pleased to know,' Bronagh continued, 'That Mrs Flaherty cooked yer woman a fresh egg, flipping it over this time and presented it to her with a smile and not so much as a sniff of a sarcastic remark.'

Air whistled through Aisling's teeth. It was a relief the breakfast cook hadn't met the request with her usual banging about in the kitchen and mutterings that would make you blush. 'I'll give her a pat on the back.' She fidgeted, moving to the window to look out for Quinn. The traffic was heavy given the wet weather, and across the road, St Stephen's Green would be quiet save for those using the park as a shortcut to get where they were going.

'It's a big day for you and Quinn,' Bronagh said, opening her drawer. 'And I don't mind telling you I'm as on edge as you are.'

The ensuing rustling told her Bronagh was into her not-so-secret biscuit stash. She watched amused as their receptionist checked over her shoulder, making sure Sara Scott wasn't lurking about before munching into it.

'It keeps my blood sugar up, Aisling,' she mumbled through her mouthful. 'The menopause plays havoc with it, so it does.' She knew better than to offer Aisling one. The only thing she could keep down in the mornings was a gingernut. A thought occurred to her. 'I wonder whether the baby will look like Ronan Keating if he's a boy?'

Aisling was saved from having to answer. The new family-friendly SUV Quinn had sheepishly brought home from the dealership a week ago had just slid into the kerb, sending up a spray of water. She rolled her eyes at the sight of the vehicle. It was her fault for telling Quinn to purchase whatever he thought would be a suitable car for them once they became a family of three. The simple reason she'd given him free rein wasn't that he was an expert in all things mechanical. He'd as much sense as she did on that front. No, it had been because she couldn't be arsed traipsing about dealerships.

However, warning bells should have sounded when Quinn informed her his two older brothers, Ivo and Rowan or Dumb and Dumber, as Aisling had nicknamed them, had offered to come with him. Desperate, she'd begged Moira's husband, Tom, to tag along and make sure Quinn didn't come home with a convertible Mustang or the like. He was a daddy himself and, as such, would ensure Quinn made a sensible purchase, she'd reassured herself. Moira had shaken her head upon hearing this, telling Aisling that there was no such thing as a sensible man when it came to cars. Her youngest sister had shown rare insight because Quinn had come home with a tank suited more to a builder than a restaurateur and guesthouse manager with one child on the way. 'Quinn's just pulled up. See you, Bronagh!'

'Good luck!' Bronagh called out as Aisling dipped her head to brave the elements outside.

Her heels tip-tapped on the slick pavement as she dodged a woman on a mission under a black umbrella to open the car's passenger door. Then, cocking a leg, Aisling heaved herself up onto the seat. 'How do you think I'm going to get in this thing when I'm nine months pregnant? I just about need a step ladder as it is. And I've my Manolo Blahnik boots on,' she directed at Quinn, whose hands were tapping the steering wheel impatiently.

Too late, she thought as the windscreen wipers swished back and forth and the indicator ticked while Quinn waited for a break in the stream of cars. She braced herself for the monologue that was sure to follow as he pulled out into the traffic.

He didn't disappoint her as he began reeling off the wagon's safety features, like the ABC song and the times tables he'd learned by rote. She tuned him out, watching the rain splatter on her window and the huddled shapes of pedestrians side-stepping puddles on the pavement as the tank crawled around the Green to turn onto Lower Baggot Street. Both their heads automatically swung towards Quinn's namesake restaurant. The door to the bistro opened, and they caught a glimpse of a suit-clad man and a woman in a smart blue coat with gold buttons exiting. An early lunch perhaps, Aisling mused.

'I hope they're satisfied diners,' Quinn said, his brow furrowed in the couple's direction.

'I'm sure they are,' Aisling reassured him, shifting in her seat, trying to get into a bladder-friendly position. 'Look there. He's loosening the waistband of his trousers. That's the mark of a satisfied customer,' she said, jabbing at the window.

Quinn laughed, and she was pleased. The restaurant was his first baby, and she knew it was hard for him to take a step back. He'd trained his staff well, and common sense told him they were perfectly able to manage the busy lunchtime service without him. But it was hard to separate common sense from passion, and he'd shed blood, sweat and tears building his business into the popular Irish bistro it was today. Despite the tug of the restaurant, her husband had put her first every time, never missing an appointment on what had turned out to be quite the pregnancy journey for them. She turned away from the window to study his profile, feeling a surge of love. She was a lucky woman to have married Quinn, who'd be a wonderful daddy.

'What?' Quinn asked and, feeling her eyes on him, glanced over.

'I was just thinking what a lovely daddy you're going to be.'

'And you're going to be the best mammy.' He reached out, picking her hand up off her lap to give it a quick squeeze before giving the road ahead of them his full attention. 'The traffic will thin out once we get onto Northumberland Road.'

Aisling was worried about whether there'd be any potholes en route, but given they were heading to Blackrock, not rural Ireland, she thought she'd probably be alright.

Her mind latched onto her latest worry. How would she and Quinn manage two demanding roles when the baby came? Tom and Moira juggled Kiera successfully, but they had a lot of help. Mammy and Tom's mam were on board. But, Maeve Moran had battled ill health in recent years and raised four boys. So, it wasn't fair to ask her to commit to helping care for her and Quinn's baby. Mammy would want to be hands-on with her new grandchild, but she already had her hands full with Kiera.

Aisling chewed her thumbnail. She knew she'd have to take a back step, cut down her hours at the very least but like Quinn, O'Mara's was her first baby.

She'd stepped in and taken over when Mammy had been unable to face continuing to run it without her husband by her side. And, by doing so, had ensured the guesthouse stayed in the family and continued to turn a profit. Moreover, she was responsible for ensuring their staff were paid. How could she trust all that to someone else?

Aisling sighed. Like the birthing of the pumpkin heads, she'd cross that bridge when she came to it.

Chapter Three

♥

The clinic Dr Kinsella had written Aisling's referral to was in a nondescript building not far from Blackrock Market and Quinn backed the tank into a parking space as close to the entrance as he could find.

'I don't know how you think I'm going to manage parking the fecking thing,' Aisling muttered, unbuckling. 'It's not far off needing a pilot vehicle with 'wide load' on it leading the way.'

'There's nothing to it, Ash. It's all in the wing mirrors,' Quinn said.

Aisling noticed his voice had dropped an octave. 'Listen to you, Testosterone Ted. And don't even think about giving me the safety rating rundown again.'

Quinn wisely kept his mouth shut and, clambering down, came around to help Aisling out of the SUV. Then with a firm grasp of her hand, they dashed for the entrance. Aisling thought it was a danger run, feeling the pressure on her poor bladder as she stomped her Manolos on the mat inside the door.

It took a moment to get their bearings in the glaringly white foyer after the gloom outside, but they saw the dark-haired receptionist smiling over at them when they did. Aisling noticed she had lipstick on her teeth as she managed a desperate smile back.

'Good morning, I'm Martina. Do you have your referral form, please?'

Aisling and Quinn nodded, the raindrops dripping off the bottom of their respective jackets. Quinn looked at Aisling, waiting for her to dig the form out, which had somehow migrated to the bottom of her handbag between leaving home and arriving at the clinic.

'Here you go.' Aisling offered an apologetic smile as she handed over the crumpled paper. Martina glanced at it and tapped something into her computer before clipping another form onto a clipboard.

'If you could fill this in and return it to me, please.' She held the clipboard out, and Quinn took it from her. Then pointing to an alcove over to the left, she added, 'You'll find the waiting room through there.'

Aisling wished she was Moira right then because Moira would have told Martina about the lipstick. Moira would also have demanded to know how long she would have to wait for her appointment, not smile meekly and walk knock-kneed behind her husband to the waiting area.

'Shall I fill it in?' Quinn asked, eager for something to do as he sat down in one of the last two seats, pen already poised over the questionnaire.

'Fine by me.' Aisling glanced around at the other women, in varying stages of pregnancy, seated alongside their partners. She wondered if they were all desperate for the loo too. Given their frowning concentration and tightly crossed legs as they flicked through magazines, she guessed they probably were.

A small boy with a matted nest of blond hair was vroom, vrooming a toy car across the carpet, and a dubious smell wafted towards them. Aisling scanned the room for suspects, her eyes settling on the plump baby girl on her mam's lap. She was the picture of innocence as she mouthed a teething ring, but her mammy was breathing through her mouth.

Quinn took the completed form back to reception and, as he sat down, told Aisling they shouldn't have to wait too long. 'Martina said the appointments are running to schedule.'

Aisling sent up a silent prayer of thanks before telling him to stop with the jiggling of the leg because it wasn't his bladder that was in danger of rupturing. She knew she'd be unable to concentrate on any of the magazines on offer and Quinn was busy making silly faces at the smelly baby, so she leant back on the seat and allowed her eyes to close. She'd taken to catnapping at any opportunity, but her mind was too busy to allow her to relax.

One day soon, she and Quinn would have to sit down and have a heart-to-heart about how they envisaged managing their work and a new baby.

Aisling was startled as Quinn nudged her. 'What?'

'Your phone.'

'Oh, I was miles away. Sorry.' She fumbled about in her bag for it, intent on switching it off. In her opinion, people who had loud conversations on their mobile phones in waiting rooms were rude. Mammy sprang to mind, and hoping it wasn't her ringing to say it wasn't too late because she could still make it to the clinic, she checked the screen quickly before switching the phone off.

'It was Leila,' she said to Quinn. 'She must have been ringing to wish us well.'

Quinn paused in his face-pulling at the baby. 'That's nice.'

It was nice, Aisling thought. Leila had been making a concerted effort to show interest in her morning sickness, constant need for the loo and penchant for gingernuts. It wasn't one-sided. Aisling made sure she listened when Leila brought up her boyfriend, Bearach because while she and Leila were at different stages in their lives, it was important not to let what was going on in your world consume you—a lesson Aisling had learned on her quest to get pregnant when they'd fallen out briefly.

A man in a crisp white coat denoting he was a medical person appeared. 'Geraldine Pritchard?'

'That's me,' a nasal voice answered. The mammy with the smelly baby got to her feet, as did the man sitting alongside her.

'Thank God for that,' the studiously dressed woman next to Aisling said once the family had disappeared down the corridor. 'They say you don't bat an eye when it comes to your own baby's poo, but that little girl's was making mine water.'

Aisling smiled then sobered, 'Ah Jaysus, imagine sitting in it like so.'

They both grimaced.

'You'd have thought one of them might have changed her before they went through like,' the woman said.

'Maybe you get immune to the smell and they didn't notice?'

Aisling and the woman simultaneously shook their heads and said, 'No,' then laughed.

'Laughing is not good. I'm fit to burst. I love your boots, by the way. Manolo's?'

Aisling, who had thighs of steel so tightly were they squeezed, nodded. She felt an instant kinship with her neighbour as with any man or woman who knew their designer shoes. 'Thanks.' She tucked her hair behind her ears as she smiled at her. She didn't look like the sorta woman who'd wear Manolo's dressed as she was in a plain maternity blouse with a suit jacket over the top and a pair of smart trousers. She'd boots on too, but they were much more sensible than Aisling's six-inch heels, and a pop-up umbrella lay on the floor next to them. Still and all, perhaps she was a killer heels sorta woman outside work hours.

The woman had her hands wrapped protectively around her bump, and Aisling guessed she must be nearly full term. Then, realising she'd been staring, burbled, 'I'm the same. I haven't been this busting since I was in primary school. Mean old Sister Rosamunde wouldn't let us go to the toilet during class.'

'Oh, that's awful.'

'It was. I wet my knickers when we were doing the quiet time reading while sitting on cushions. So I stayed inside at lunchtime and tried to dry myself off on the radiators. I was steaming and the smell!' Too much information, Aisling she told herself, but the other woman laughed.

'Sorry, it's funny, but it's not funny if you know what I mean. I'm Jodie, by the way. Is this your first?'

Aisling elbowed Quinn, who she sensed was about to insert himself into the conversation now he'd lost his audience. But, this was exclusive future mammy-to-mammy bonding time, and she was gratified when he got up and began rifling through the toybox.

'Yes, yours?'

Jodie nodded too. 'I'm due in two weeks, and I feel enormous.'

'Ah, sure, you're all bump.'

Jodie smiled, then glanced at her watch with a frown. 'My husband should be here any minute. He's meeting me from work, but the traffic's terrible.

'It always is when it rains,' Aisling said. 'I don't know where everybody comes from.'

The two women chatted away about morning sickness, the awful fatigue and how iron tablets gave you terrible constipation before Jodie moved on, mentioning she lived in the sought-after suburb of Sallynoggin and worked as an accountant in the city. The latter didn't come as a surprise. Her attire had hinted at her doing something that involved an office. Aisling informed her she had an older sister who worked in London for an accountancy firm.

'What do you do?' Jodie asked.

'I manage my family's guesthouse. O'Mara's. It's opposite St Stephen's Green. We live in the apartment at the top along with my sister, Moira, her partner Tom and their baby, Kiera, who's nine months. She's gorgeous.'

'I know it. I walk past it often on my way to and from the office. So, you'll have had plenty of hands-on practise then?'

Aisling nodded, and the conversation came to a lull. Jodie pressed her lips together as though weighing up whether she should say something or not. In the end, she must have decided to voice her fears because, lowering her voice, she confided, 'To be honest, I'm worried about how I'll cope with the chaos of a new baby when I'm so used to order at work and home. I've three months of maternity leave, but then I'll have to return to work. We've not long bought our first home. And I've no clue how that will work either because child care's so expensive and both our parents have busy lives. It all feels a little overwhelming.'

'Really? You look very capable.'

Jodie laughed. 'Sensible, you mean?'

Aisling opened her mouth to dig herself out, but Jodie held a hand up, 'It's alright, I know what you mean, but don't let this,' she swept a hand over her office wear, 'fool you because I might know my sums but when it comes to baby's I haven't a clue.'

It was nice to know she wasn't the only one worrying about how she'd juggle all the changes their jelly bean would bring. 'Neither have I.' Aisling glanced to where Quinn was now racing a toy car alongside the little boy and lowered her voice. 'I mean, I know how to do the practical things, but I don't know how we will manage. Quinn runs a restaurant which isn't nine to five, and the guesthouse is demanding.'

'Would you like to catch up for a coffee sometime after this one here's born?' She dipped her head towards her stomach. 'Scratch that, herbal tea. I don't know any other first-time mams or mams-to-be, and I'm not a mother-baby group sort of person.'

'I'd like that,' Aisling said, a warm glow at having made a potential new friend settling over her.

Jodie was already pulling an address book from her handbag. She opened it to A and jotted Aisling's name and number down. She'd no sooner put it back in her bag when the door to the clinic burst open, and a man in a business suit appeared, shaking himself off like a dog at the beach. Martina gave him a disapproving glare.

'That's my husband, Luke,' Jodie said, waving out to him. He strode through to the waiting area apologising for being late.

'It's alright. I haven't been seen yet. Luke, this is Aisling and—'

'Quinn Moran,' Quinn looked up from the picture book he'd been flicking through, smiling and nodding to them both.

However, there was no time for chit-chatting because a woman in a white coat had appeared. 'Jodie Trimball?'

'Good luck,' Aisling said as Jodie hauled herself out of the chair and waddled down the adjacent corridor.

Ten minutes later, Aisling found herself in a small room with unadorned cream walls and a curtain separating a desk area, home to complicated computer equipment, from the bed on which she was lying. She'd undone her jeans and bunched her sweater under her bra as per Sofia, their sonographer's instructions and Quinn, perched on a chair on the wall side of the bed, was holding her hand. Opposite him, Sofia had begun to move what she'd just explained was a transducer across the slick of gel she'd applied to Aisling's abdomen. She'd already run through what they could expect from today's examination.

Quinn's and Aisling's eyes were fixed on the grainy screen on the video console.

'I'm going to apply a little bit of pressure, Aisling, so let me know if it gets uncomfortable.'

'We will,' Quinn said, and Aisling silenced him with a look.

Sofia smiled. 'We're used to enthusiastic fathers-to-be.'

Aisling had nearly forgotten her earlier desperation for the loo in her excitement at being only seconds away from seeing their little jelly bean. Still, as Sofia pushed down harder on her lower abdomen with the transducer, she gave a sharp intake of breath. 'I'm fine,' she quickly reassured the sonographer, not wanting her to stop what she was doing. 'Just in need of a visit to the jacks is all.'

'Jacks?' Sofia enquired, eyebrow raised. 'I'm Romanian, and I've been in Dublin for over a year now, and I still find new Irish words I don't understand.'

'Em, Ladies.'

The sonographer nodded. 'Yes, I can see the bladder is full.' She began rotating the transducer in the same spot. 'Here we are.'

Quinn squeezed Aisling's hand so tight it almost hurt. Tears sprang as she stared at the screen. The baby's heart was beating steadily, and she saw a tiny arm that looked like it was waving at them. 'Hello, little jelly bean.' They both breathed, in awe of what they were seeing.

'Look here,' Sofia pointed to the screen. The baby just turned. Oh!'

Aisling half sat up, using her elbows for props. Quinn too had straightened anxiously. They spoke over the top of one another.

'What is it?'

'Is everything okay?'

Chapter Four

♥

'Twins,' Quinn said.

'Twins,' Aisling echoed.

They'd climbed back in the tank and were still parked outside the clinic. The smell of wet wool clung to them, and the rain was sheeting down the windscreen, obscuring their view. Outside had faded into oblivion as they tried to process what the ultrasound had revealed. The whole thing had taken under forty minutes, including Aisling's visit to the toilet immediately after her tummy had been wiped clean of the gel. Forty minutes and the world as they knew it had just tilted on its axis.

'It's amazing,' Quinn said.

'A miracle,' Aisling added.

Quinn reached over for her hand and she took it as though he'd offered her a lifeline. The proof that she was carrying not one jelly bean but two was tucked inside the manilla folder on her lap. It was irrefutable evidence.

'It's scary,' Quinn said, voicing what Aisling was thinking. 'Two babies. Two of everything.'

'Double trouble, and it's terrifying.' She nodded. 'And exciting.'

'Very exciting.'

'We're going to be the parents of twins,' Aisling repeated, needing to keep saying the word so it would sink in.

'The proud parents,' Quinn corrected. 'I know. It's mad.' He leant over and kissed his wife. 'I love you, Mrs O'Mara-Moran.' He gave her hand a reassuring squeeze.

'I love you too, Mr Moran.'

Quinn fidgeted behind the wheel. 'I've got all this nervous energy. I want to run down Grafton Street tapping strangers on the shoulder to tell them we're after having twins. Or, I don't know,'—he shrugged—'storm a radio station and broadcast it.'

Aisling laughed, knowing what he meant. 'Me too.'

'What should we do now? Because obviously, we can't accost strangers and take over the airwaves. There's no point going for a drink to celebrate, given I'd have to drink all the bubbles. Actually—'

'Don't mention bubbles!' Aisling reached for a gingernut from the container she never left home without these days. The thought of alcohol, especially fizzy alcohol, had brought on a wave of nausea. Her forehead was clammy, and her skin was hot despite her damp clothes. She chomped the biscuit down, hoping the sick feeling would pass, before resting her head on the seat and closing her eyes. Her breath came in short huffs. Quinn knew from experience that the best thing he could do in these circumstances was nothing, so he happily passed the minutes until Aisling announced she was alright by fiddling with all the knobs on the dashboard.

'We should go and see Mammy and Donal,' Aisling said, sitting forward and quickly adding, 'And we can go straight over to Blanchardstown to give your mam and dad the news afterwards.' Quinn was very tolerant of his mammy-in-law's need to be the first in the know, and it was just as well Maeve Moran had a placid nature. 'It's a lot of driving, I know, but sure, it's not the sort of thing we can tell them over the phone.

And besides, I want to see their expressions when they find out they're getting two grandbabies for one.'

'Me too.'

'We'll let everyone else know the good news later.' Because it was good news, Aisling reassured herself as she tried to visualise feeding two babies simultaneously.

'That sounds like a good plan, and it'll give the car a decent run,' Quinn conceded, fishing his mobile out of his jacket pocket. 'I'll ring Tony and tell him I won't be back until this evening's dinner service.'

'And I'd best give Bronagh a call,' Aisling added for her benefit as much as Quinn's, 'Just say it went well if Tony asks how we got on, alright?' Of course, Bronagh would want a blow-by-blow account of the ultrasound. It wasn't going to be easy keeping quiet.

'My lips are sealed,' Quinn said. They turned away from each other to make their calls. His chat with his trusty sous chef was over in seconds and the tank rumbled into life as he turned the key in the ignition. He flicked on the windscreen wipers, shaking his head hearing Aisling assuring Bronagh that she wasn't hiding anything.

'It all went well, Bronagh, everything's as it should be. I'll show you the picture of the jelly bean tomorrow. I promise.' Aisling held the phone away from her ear as Bronagh pressed her for more information. She was like Mammy insomuch as she had a sixth sense when it came to not getting the whole story. 'Bronagh, you're cutting out, sorry. I'm going to hang up. I'll speak to you tomorrow.' She disconnected the call.

'Is that what you do to me when you're in Brown Thomas?' Quinn asked, referencing the department store Aisling was fond of shopping in when she found time.

Aisling smiled. 'The reception's terrible in there, so it is.'

'And is it bad in Arnotts and Debenhams too?'

'Very bad.' A question occurred to her as they exited the car park. 'Is there a history of twins in your family?

'No. Not so far as I know. Yours?'

'No.'

They lapsed into silence and Aisling stared out the window, thinking about Jodie and wondering how her scan had gone. She wished she'd got her number because she would have liked to have rung her and told her about their unexpected news. The tank slowed and stopped at the lights five minutes into their journey. Her attention was caught by a mother getting soaked as she wrestled a young child into the back seat of her parked car. The tot was arching her back in presumed protest at being put in her car seat. Her heart began to beat faster. 'Quinn?'

'Hmm?' He drummed the steering wheel impatiently.

'How will I manage when the babies are toddlers, and I've to put them in the car. How will I keep hold of one while I put the other in their seat? How will I keep them safe?' Her throat began to feel like it was closing over.

'Breathe, Ash.'

She took a couple of gulps of air and might have found his masterfulness attractive under different circumstances. But it was highly likely that his masterfulness got her into this situation in the first place. He'd a particular way of saying, 'Do you feel like a ride tonight?' That always saw her trot off to the boudoir.

'Listen to me, alright? We've only just found out we're having twins. So don't get ahead of yourself worrying about how we'll get on because we will manage. You do, don't you, when you have to?'

Aisling nodded slightly. 'Jaysus, Quinn, what about the potty training?'

Quinn laughed. 'Ash, people have twins all the time. Sure, we'll figure it out as we go. Okay?'

She nodded, feeling calmer. 'Okay.' Her phone rang again.

'It's a hotline you're running there today.' Quinn cast a sideways glance at Aisling as she dug out her phone.

'It's Rosi,' Aisling said. Her eldest sister had telephoned her the night before to wish her all the best for the scan and would be wanting an update. 'I'll answer it.' She hit the button. 'How're you, Rosi?'

'I'm at work, and Norman's in a right mood on account of the, erm, accounts he's doing not adding up, so I can't talk long, but I wanted to see how you and Quinn got on.'

Aisling squirmed. She was desperate to spill the beans. It had taken a herculean effort not to tell Bronagh, who'd be thrilled at the prospect of two little babbies but it wasn't worth the wrath of Mammy or, worse, a wounded Mammy. Roisin was her sister, though. Surely that gave her special sibling rights?'

Quinn prodded her leg, and she glanced over at him.

'Don't,' he mouthed.

She did and then held the phone away from her ear so as not to be deafened by Roisin's squeals of delight.

'That will come back and bite you in the arse,' Quinn muttered.

Once Roisin had calmed down, apologising to her startled workmates, she said, 'I'll design you a yoga plan to get your hip flexors used to being stretched for the labour like. Ooh, Ash, it's so exciting!'

Aisling would rather stick pins in her eyes than do the yoga.

'Of course, you'll need all the help you can get for birthing twins, so the more stretching between now and then, the better.'

'Thanks a million,' Aisling said. 'We're on our way to Howth now to tell Mammy and Donal the news, so don't be letting on I spoke to you first. You know what she's like.'

'I won't breathe a word. I promise. I can't believe it! Wait until Moira finds out.'

They chatted about birth, babies and the like, with Roisin seemingly having forgotten she was on a personal call during work hours. Then, in an abrupt change of subject, Roisin asked, 'Ash, I don't suppose Mammy told you my news, did she?'

Aisling was on high alert. 'No. I spoke to her this morning too. She was making a last-ditch attempt at coming to the scan, but I held firm. Come to think of it, she did ring me back, but I didn't answer. Jaysus wept, Rosi, you're not pregnant, are you?'

Quinn's eyebrows shot up into his hairline. That would be a turn-up. Shay's musician lifestyle would be in for a shock if he were to become a daddy.

'Feck off away with you. I am not and don't be saying that sorta thing around Shay either. Neither of us is ready for that. I am, however, a grandmother as of this morning.'

'She's not pregnant, Quinn.' Aisling reassured him. 'But she is a grandmother.'

Quin shook his head. They were a mad lot, the O'Maras.

'Steve's after giving birth this morning to eight baby gerbils. Noah says they're called pups.'

'Steve, as in the gerbil, Mr Nibbles was after bullying?'

'The one and same.'

'I don't believe it.' Aisling turned to Quinn, who kept darting little glances her way as he tried to keep track of what was going on. 'Steve the gerbil's given birth.'

The eyebrows shot up in his head once more.

'It turns out Steve should have been called Stef,' Roisin elaborated.

'He's a she,' Aisling explained, conjuring up a disturbing image from Rosi and Noah's last visit. 'So when we all thought Mr Nibbles was bullying Steve by sitting on him, he was actually—'

'Precisely. Mr Nibbles was getting up to the gerbil shenanigans with Steve.'

'While we all stood around watching.' Aisling shuddered. 'But how did you not notice Steve was Stef in the first place.'

'I don't know, tis a mystery, Sure we only noticed Steve was looking plump two days ago. He was acting strangely. Well, stranger than normal, gathering all the shredded paper in the cage into a pile, but we didn't put two and two together. The lady gerbils have a very short gestation period. But that's not the worst of it either. While Noah and I ate our cornflakes, Mr Nibbles was only at it again this morning. I was about to go and get a glass of cold water to toss over him when Noah read in his gerbil guide that it's normal behaviour for them to mate again straight after the female delivers her litter. So, we should expect another surprise in twenty-five days. Christ on a bike Aisling, I could be in for sixteen of the little feckers. What am I going to do with them all?'

Aisling could just about see her sister tearing her hair at her desk.

'It's simple, Rosi. Colin introduced Steve to Mr Nibbles; therefore, it's Colin's problem? Moira will tell you the same thing.'

'Mammy did too, and you're right, but it's easier said than done. Noah's after earmarking two of the pups already. One for Kiera and one for your new baby. He'll be delighted to choose another for you when I tell him the news. And, I'll make sure he checks their bits and bobs properly, so you don't wind up in the same predicament as we have. And, of course, he wants to keep the rest of them. It was a battle to get him to leave them this morning, and he was late for school.'

'Rosi!'

'What?'

'I am going to be the mother of twins. I don't want gerbils to boot. I'm sure Moira and Tom will be with us on that one.'

'Well, you'll have to tell Noah yourselves because it's going to be hard enough for him when he has to wave the rest of the pups off.' Roisin's tone suddenly changed, 'Yes, no problem, Mr Langmore. I'll fax the invoice through to you straight away. Alright then, stand by. Cheerio.'

The phone went dead.

'Can you believe that?' Aisling shoved her phone back into her bag. 'She's only after trying to fob three of the baby gerbils off to us and Moira and Tom as pets for the babbies'

Quinn could well believe it. 'You shouldn't have told her our news until we'd been to see your mam and Donal, Ash.'

'She promised she won't say anything.'

'When have any of you been able to keep anything to yourself. Roisin being point in case.'

Aisling couldn't argue with him.

The rain was being pushed away by a strong sea breeze when the tank reached the Howth road, and the sun was putting up a valiant effort to shine, giving the sky a stormy hue. Aisling thought that it wasn't dissimilar to Mammy's cushion arrangement on her sofa, seeing a rainbow arcing through the clouds and hovering over the sea. She leant forward, noticing something else. It was only faint, but it was there. 'Look,' she pointed out to sea with a note of wonder in her voice.

'It's a rainbow, Ash,' Quinn stated, nonplussed. It wasn't exactly an unusual sight in Ireland.

'It's not just a rainbow. Look again.'

Quinn did so, and a grin slowly spread across his face as the second twin arch Aisling had spotted grew more intense in colour. 'A double rainbow,' he said softly.

'It's a sign, so it is.' Aisling said, settling back into her seat and placing her hands on her tummy. Everything would be alright.

Chapter Five

♥

'Don't even think about it, Quinn! Sure, you're to be a daddy soon. A man of responsibility.' Aisling had seen her husband's leg tense and knew he was itching to put his foot down on the accelerator as they turned onto Mornington Mews' gravelled driveway. 'Mammy will have your guts for garters if you pull up pretending you're in the Grand Prix like Moira's apt to do.'

Quinn gunned the engine, torn. 'It's the sound of the wheels on the gravel, Ash. It brings out something primal in me.'

Quick as a flash, Aisling responded, 'Cop on to yourself. It's you bringing out something primal that has us coming around to tell Mammy and Donal they're going to be the grandparents of twins.'

So it was, instead of skidding up to the front door of the end townhouse in a blaze of gravel, the tank grumbled to a sedate standstill. Amanda from the middle house in the trio of converted townhouses that had once been a grand Edwardian manor looked up. She was trimming her topiary bush and gave them an approving hello wave. Aisling held her hand up in response. Quinn stilled the engine, and the door to the house swung open before they'd had a chance to unbuckle their seat belts.

Maureen was a vision in the hot pink fitted sweat top she'd teemed with her Mo-pants and the hot pink slippers Moira had given her last Mother's Day. At least she wasn't wearing the matching pink bottoms, Aisling thought. That Ciara at Mammy's favourite fashion boutique in Howth had a lot to answer for. Namely, her Mammy looking like a geriatric Eva Longoria from *Desperate Housewives* in her activewear which she was very keen on telling anyone who'd listen, was all the go these days.

'Jaysus, she does have the sixth sense,' Quinn said, shivering. 'It's spooky.'

'I told you' Aisling said, hurriedly disembarking. She made her way over to the front step and heard Mammy saying a crisp hello to her neighbour. She wasn't as keen to curry favour with the posh Amanda and Terence these days. Not since learning at the housewarming party thrown at the end of summer the couple had a penchant for swinging. The memory of Mammy's face when she'd realised it was more than gin and tonics in the garden with her and Donal that the neighbours had in mind, coupled with the hula dancing entertainment that had gone spectacularly wrong that night, still made Aisling smile. The Howth housewarming party was one nobody would forget in a hurry.

Amid mutterings of, Did they think it was an entire hurling team they would be shepherding to the Saturday matches in six months or a baby, as she clocked the tank, Maureen swept Aisling and Quinn into the house. The door was closed behind them before Amanda could ask how they were.

'Mammy, that was rude.'

'It's your best interests I've got at heart, Aisling. I wouldn't put it past her to dangle the pineapple key ring at you and Quinn if you hang about outside too long.' She barely drew breath as her daughter and son-in-law wiped their shoes on the mat. 'You're lucky you've caught us. We've just returned from taking Kiera down to see the big Christmas tree in

Howth. We'd have been back sooner, only we ran into Bold Brenda, who was after Tom's phone number. She said she's a friend needing a bartender for a private party.' Maureen made the inverted commas sign with her index fingers.

Aisling cringed. It was an annoying habit Maureen had picked up of late; that and talk to the hand. The nose tapping for mind your own business was still the most annoying of all, though.

'She said how impressed she was with his cocktail-making skills at the housewarming and how he was very good with his hands. I told her what did she expect? He's a doctor in training and far too busy for the private party malarky.'

'Moira and Tom could probably do with the extra money, Maureen,' Quinn said, taking his jacket off and hanging it up. Aisling did the same.

'Quinn Moran, no son-in-law of mine is going to be hiring himself out for Bold Brenda's friends' private parties, thank you very much.' Maureen sniffed. 'So think on.' She registered the folder Aisling had hold of. 'Are those the photographs from the ultrasound?'

Aisling held the folder aloft as Maureen lunged for it. 'They are, and I'll show you them in a minute, Mammy.'

'I thought you were going to telephone to tell me how it went. Why have you called around?' A note of hysteria crept in. 'Is everything alright?'

'Slow down.' For someone averse to her mammy's hand language, Aisling held hers up in a stop sign. 'Everything's grand, Mammy. We wanted to show you the pictures is all. They're very clear, so they are. And sure, since when do we need an invitation to call in for a cup of tea?' Aisling didn't hang about for an answer as she tottered towards the open-plan living room.

Maureen's voice echoed after her, 'Aisling O'Mara, you're with child, you know, which means you should—'

Aisling froze in the doorway to the living room, and Quinn nearly went into the back of her. She spun around, looking past her husband at her mammy, 'O'Mara-Moran, Mammy, and don't be saying 'with child' like so, Mammy. It makes me sound like the Virgin Mary. Quinn did have a part to play in the conception.'

'There's no show of virgin anything with my girls,' Maureen muttered, and Quinn smirked. 'Or with those boots you've got on either, my girl. Holy Mother of God, Aisling, you could take someone's eye out with the heels on them! You're hardly going to be able to prance about the place in those now, are you? Not when you start showing. Sure, you'd overbalance and wind up flat on your face, and that wouldn't be good for the poor little babby. It's just as well I've got contacts because what I was going to say was, why don't you and I pay a visit to Carrick's? We'll get you sorted with a more suitable pair for a woman in your condition.'

'Yer Chinky the pixie shoe man, you mean?'

'No.' Maureen frowned. 'His name's Cathal and he's a cobbler.'

'Mammy, I don't want special boots like Rosemary Farrell.'

Maureen's lips tightened. 'I'm telling you, Aisling, what that man can't do with a cutter, leather and thread isn't worth doing. You're the mother of my grandchild. He's sure to give you a discount.'

Aisling scowled, almost forgetting their visit's purpose by the time she swung back to greet Donal and Kiera. They were sitting on the floor building a brick tower. Or at least Donal was doing the building as he stacked the numbered bricks counting out one, two, three, four. Kiera was poised to knock the tower down but forgot the bricks and gave her aunt and uncle a two-toothed grin instead.

Aisling and Quinn grinned back at her. It was impossible not to.

Donal placed the last block on the tower and then began rocking back and forth, reminding Aisling of a turtle on its back trying to right itself as he greeted Aisling and Quinn.

'Don't get up, Donal,' Aisling said, trying not to giggle.

'Chance would be a fine thing,' Maureen said, standing beside the Christmas tree. It was a real one, giving off a piney aroma and had been put up two days before on the eighth of December as tradition dictated on the Feast of the Immaculate Conception. She smiled fondly down at her live-in man friend. 'Sure, I've to bend my knees and heave him up or he'd be down there all day, so he would.'

'You're not far wrong there, Maureen,' Donal said, his eyes creasing at the corners as he smiled good-naturedly at his lady love. 'How're you two?' he directed towards Aisling and Quinn. 'This is a nice surprise, so it is.'

'They've brought the scan photos for us to see, Donal.' She rubbed her hands together. ''Tis very exciting.'

'We're grand,' Aisling answered for both of them. 'Mammy probably told you we were after having our first ultrasound this morning?'

'She did mention it once or twice.' Donal's eyes twinkled, and Aisling smiled. Poor Donal had probably had a proper ear-bashing over her not being allowed to attend the scan.

'So, we thought we'd call by for a cuppa and show you the pictures. The tree looks lovely, by the way.' Aisling knew there'd been heated debate as to whether they get a real tree or use Mammy's pretend one that had served her proudly for as long as she could remember. 'The needles make a mess,' she'd argued, but Donal had won. He was good for her mammy, was Donal, Aisling thought, turning to her. 'I'm gasping, so I am.' Quinn would be too after the morning they'd had.

'I like a real tree,' Donal said. 'You can't beat the smell.'

Maureen bent to pick up a handful of pine needles.

The house was a cosy respite after the diabolical weather they'd faced earlier, Aisling thought as the flames danced in the gas fire, inviting her over. She moved towards it to warm her backside, feeling Mammy's beady-eyed gaze on the folder as Quinn joined her. She tightened her grip on it because she wouldn't put it past her to make another grab for it. In the background, Kenny Rogers was crooning 'She Believes in Me'. Aisling sniffed the air. She could even smell something over the Christmassy pine that she was sure she would find delicious under normal circumstances. She deduced that her mam must have her and Donal's dinner bubbling in the crockpot. As for Pooh, he was stretched out on the mat by the French doors looking very chilled with his poodly head resting on his paws.

'How're you, Pooh?' Quinn called over. He was fond of the poodle, and Aisling knew he'd gun for a puppy one of these days. Though how a puppy would work at O'Mara's, she didn't know. Gerbils would be easier to manage.

Pooh lifted his head and ruff-ruffed his greeting but didn't move, and Aisling looked past the poodle to the view of Howth Harbour beyond. It was hard to see where the sea met the sky today.

'I had to put the Kenny Rogers CD on to distract him from the flip-flops,' Maureen explained. 'Kiera likes it too. Don't you poppet?'

Kiera smacked the brick tower sending the bricks toppling, and gave a high-pitched squeal, making them all wince.

'Ah no! Not again, Kiera!' Donal pretended to be aghast, and Kiera giggled.

Her niece reminded Aisling of Moira at that moment, and Poppa D, the name that had been settled on for Donal where Maureen's grandchildren were concerned, had the patience of a saint. She watched him sweep the bricks up to stack them once more. Mind you, he had to, living with Mammy.

Maureen held her hand out, wiggling her fingers. 'C'mon, I'd like to see my future grandchild. Not that I should have had to wait. I should have been right there for the live screening, so I should.'

'Ah, Mammy, don't be giving out. Can't we have a cup of tea first?'

'And a sandwich, Mo?' Donal asked hopefully.

Maureen hesitated. She'd been about to make lunch when Aisling and Quinn had arrived.

'It's time for Kiera's lunch, isn't it?' Aisling said, glancing at the wall clock in the kitchen.

'She'll scream blue murder if her food isn't served up within five minutes, Mo,' Donal added.

Maureen knew he was right. Her granddaughter had taken to the solids like a duck to water. She'd a hearty appetite and Maureen was sure, given half a chance, she'd be putting her hand up for the meat and three veg. She was proud of this, given Rosemary Farrell's grandchildren were picky eaters. There was a list as long as her arm stuck on her fridge with who wouldn't eat what.

'You don't want to rush looking through these, Mam.' Aisling flapped the folder.

'Aisling!' Quinn frowned, snatching them from her. 'You'll bend them.'

'Quinn's getting hungry and all, Mammy. He always gets fractious when he needs to eat.'

'How does a ham sandwich sound?' Maureen asked Quinn, who beamed his response. 'Aisling?'

'Just a cup of tea for me.'

'You've got to eat, Aisling. Could you not get a piece of dry toast down yer?'

'She's right, Ash,' Quinn said.

'Who's she, the cat's mother?'

'Sorry.' Quinn apologised to his mammy-in-law and corrected himself, 'Maureen's right.'

Aisling supposed they had a point. She was eating for three, after all.

'A slice of dry toast then, please, Mammy and not the crust. I don't like the crust, and my hair's curly enough, thank you.'

'One slice of dry toast, three ham sandwiches and a pottle of vegetable puree coming right up.' Maureen rustled off to the kitchen while Aisling and Quinn made themselves comfortable.

'How's Louise and the family getting on?' Aisling asked Donal.

'Grand. We're going to them on Christmas morning.'

'And Anna?'

'She'll be joining us with Helen.'

Aisling smiled. She knew it had been a shock initially for Donal to find out his younger child was gay but fair play to him because he'd welcomed Helen into the family fold without so much as a bat of his eyelid.

It would have meant a lot to Mammy to have her family around her this Christmas, with it being Kiera's first. But the way it was shaping up, it would be just Tom, Moira and Kiera fronting up for their dinner. As for Roisin, she had to spend it with her ex and his mother this year, and there'd been no mention of Pat and Cindy winging their way over. In years gone by, Christmas dinner was held in the dining room of O'Mara's, which meant covering reception was never a problem. However, this year would be different because not only were Mammy and Donal hosting it here in Howth, but Bronagh had booked time off, and as such, it looked like Aisling would be on call.

'A card from your Great Aunty Noreen came today, Aisling. It's on the mantle,' Maureen called from the kitchen. 'How's Freya getting on?'

'She's settling in well, Mammy.' Aisling's mind drifted to the dark-haired young woman she'd been talking about with Bronagh earlier. They'd both agreed she was proving herself to be indispensable. It was strange to think how she'd been reluctant to take her on, given Freya's mam, Emer, was the rotten egg of the family. She'd thought the apple didn't fall far from the tree, but Mammy had twisted her arm, saying everybody deserved a chance, especially family. Sure, Freya was doing a hotel and hospitality course here in Dublin, and it would be an opportunity for her to learn the ropes first-hand, she'd urged. So, in the end, Aisling relented and gave her a go. She'd not regretted it.

'Grand.'

Five minutes later, they were seated around the table. The others tucked into their sandwiches while Aisling fed Kiera the mustardy-coloured puree and nibbled on her toast. She smiled as Kiera smacked her lips together, sending specks of yellow flying. It was just as well Mammy had a plastic sheet down under the high chair, she thought.

'Watch her, Aisling,' Maureen warned. 'She'll have the hand off yer if you're not careful.'

When Aisling turned towards her mammy to tell her she knew what she was doing, thanks very much, Kiera smacked her fist down into the Beatrix Potter bowl. Globs of pureed vegetables splattered all over Aisling while Kiera grinned angelically.

Aisling sat frozen with Kiera's lunch congealing in her hair, while Maureen leapt into action to sponge her sweater. She was poised with the sponge at the ready as her daughter broke into sobs.

Chapter Six

♥

A cup of tea with a hefty dollop of sugar had restored Aisling's equilibrium, and she was sitting on the sofa next to Quinn in a yellow version of Maureen's hot pink sweat top. She suspected it made her skin look green as she gave her nose one final blow and smiled at Quinn, communicating her excitement at being about to share their unexpected news. He grinned back, taking hold of her hand and squeezing it.

Her sweater and hair had been dealt with by Mammy, who'd blamed the tears on hormones. Hormones and being over- whelmed by having seen her baby for the first time. Both were true, but Aisling and Quinn knew something Maureen didn't and Aisling's fear of how she'd manage spoon-feeding two babies when she couldn't even manage one would be brought up later with Quinn.

Kiera's wails from the spare bedroom where her port-a-cot was permanently erected had dropped several decibels. Mau- reen knew from experience that she'd succumb to her after- noon nap any minute. Kiera was overwrought, having joined in with her aunty's sobs, startled by her sudden outburst.

Maureen thought Donal a very capable man as she joined him by the fireside, the flames flickering behind them. He'd soothed Kiera while Maureen tended to Aisling, and Quinn helped himself to another sandwich from the plate in the middle of the table. Then Donal had heated up more of Maureen's homemade vegetable medley and had finished giving the babby lunch. She linked her arm through his, feeling like a lucky woman as she looked over at her daughter and son-in-law. The anticipation of the grand scan reveal was palpable but as Aisling and Quinn grinned inanely at each other, Maureen grew fidgety, and Donal draped a beefy arm around her shoulder.

Quinn was holding the folder, and with his smile reaching both ears, he asked, 'Do you want to do it, Ash?'

'You're grand. Go ahead.'

'No, I'll have my turn at my mam and dad's later.'

Maureen shook Donal off and took a step towards them. 'Would one of you open the yoke before I come over and do it myself! You're beginning to get on my last nerve.'

'Stay where you are, Mammy.' Aisling did the stop sign. 'I'll do it.' She took charge of the folder and opened it, dragging out removing the scans inside as though she were removing a glove during a striptease.

Maureen, whose face had turned the same shade as her tracksuit top, was just about pawing at the ground and snorting by the time Aisling had discarded the folder. She carefully held the ultrasounds by their edges as she looked towards her mammy and Donal. 'You might want to sit down.'

'We're grand, thank you all the same.' Maureen clasped her hands in front of her chest as though in prayer. A hot pink Madonna.

'Okay. Well, as we told you. The scan went well,' Aisling began.

'But it did show up something surprising,' Quinn continued.

Maureen was beside herself. 'You're putting me in mind of the *Two Ronnies*.'

'It's a goodnight from me, and it's a goodnight from him,' Donal deadpanned. He received a withering look for his efforts from Maureen.

'Would you spit it out or I won't be responsible for my actions!'

'We're having twins!' Aisling and Quinn chimed.

'Sweet Mother of Divine! I need to sit down.' Maureen staggered over to the armchair and collapsed into it. 'Donal, did you hear what they just said? It's two memory quilts I'll be making.'

Donal's smile was high wattage, and they heard Kiera give a random shriek from the spare bedroom. Aisling doubted it was over the news she was to have two new cousins.

'I did indeed, Mo. It's grand news, so!' He took a step towards the parents-to-be who hastily set the scans to one side.

Maureen was not going to let Donal be first in the congratulatory hugs stakes, and as though a rocket had been placed under her chair, she bounced out of it, all but knocking him aside to get to her daughter.

'Congratulations, the pair of you.' Donal made for Quinn instead, giving his hand a hearty shake.

'It's a shock, Mammy,' Aisling said, being pulled to her feet and into a bosomy, Arpège embrace. 'But it's a good one, of course. I won't say I'm not worried about how we'll cope with two of them, though.'

Maureen squeezed her tight. 'It's a miracle is what it is, Aisling. Sure, I'm to be the nana of twins!' Just wait until she told Rosemary Farrell! 'And, you and Quinn won't have to manage by yourselves. You've us and the Morans. If I know Maeve, she'll be only too eager to help out. That's what family is for, Aisling.' Then leaving Aisling to be swallowed up in a congratulatory hug from Donal, Maureen moved on to Quinn, patting his cheek. 'Do you know, Quinn, I don't mind telling you I was beginning to worry about your little swimmers but sure, look it, you've made two babies with them!' He, too, was hugged so tightly he was gasping for air. 'And we're the first to know,' she said, finally releasing him. It was a statement, not a question, but Aisling and Quinn nodded emphatically. 'Well, let's see them,' Maureen demanded before glancing wildly about the room.

'They're on top of your head, Maureen.' Donal tapped his head.

'What would I do without you, Donal?' Maureen said, sliding her glasses on. She gazed up at the first scan Aisling was holding up to the light, thinking it was hard to tell what she was supposed to be looking at.

'This one here's the best, Mammy. You can see them both clear as day. Look.'

All four of them stared mesmerised at the image of two babies.

'Tis a miracle.' Maureen repeated her earlier sentiment. 'This calls for the good biscuits, so it does. I've some chocolate-covered ginger ones in for you, Aisling.'

'I'll make us another pot of tea,' Donal offered as Kiera made them aware she wasn't settling with another squeal.

'The little monkey knows she's missing out,' Maureen said. 'I might as well fetch her up. Moira will be here in half an hour, and there's no point in her dropping off now. She'll sleep for her mammy in the car.'

Donal banged about fetching the tea things in the kitchen, and Quinn went to give him a hand while Maureen disappeared, returning seconds later with a red-cheeked Kiera. The little girl gave her aunt a delirious and victorious smile before Maureen thrust her at Aisling. 'Here. You can tell her the good news while I work out what time it is in Los Angeles. I need my fingers, so.' She sat down in the armchair.

Aisling hyped Kiera further by jiggling her on her knee in a pretend horsey ride while Maureen counted out the eight-hour time difference on her fingers. She concluded it should be a good time to phone Patrick with Aisling's news. Moira would find out first-hand soon enough; of course, Roisin would have to be rung too.

Donal presented them with a mug of tea, and Quinn did a round with the biscuit tin.

'You can't beat a chocolate digestive,' Donal remarked, settling himself down, and a murmur of agreement sounded.

'Mammy, can Kiera have a biscuit?'

Kiera was reaching for Aisling's.

'I don't see why not. Just don't be telling Moira.'

Quinn handed Kiera a digestive and she stared at it for the marvellous thing it was before jamming it in her mouth. Aisling set her down on the floor.

Maureen went to fetch the phone, announcing, 'We'll ring your brother and sister with the news.'

'Ah, Mammy, we can ring Rosi later. You don't want her getting into trouble at work for the personal phone calls.'

Maureen returned, phone in hand. 'Why're you looking so shifty?'

Aisling refused to meet Quinn's gaze. 'I'm not.'

'You are. Aisling looks shifty, doesn't she, Donal?'

Donal pretended he had a mouthful rather than be forced to take sides.

'I'm not. Sure g'won, ring her, Mammy.'

Maureen hit speed dial. They all held their breath waiting for her to speak. 'Roisin, it's me. Your mammy. No, I'm not on the mobile. I'm at home and listen, Aisling and Quinn are here. They called around straight after their appointment this morning because they were told something very exciting.'

'I'll tell her, Mammy,' Aisling said, reaching out for the phone, but Maureen was having none of it, putting the phone on speaker in time for them all to hear Roisin ask, 'What were they told, Mammy?'

'Roisin, would you believe it? They're after having triplets.'

Roisin shrieked and there was a clattering and a scuffle before she came back. 'I dropped the phone. I don't understand, Mammy. Aisling told me she's having twins. Not triplets. Are you sure you're after hearing, right?'

'Thanks a million, Rosi, you eejit,' Aisling called out.

'The first to know, were we?' Maureen said, lips pursed.

Quinn mouthed, 'I told you so,' at Aisling and received a scowl. She knew the only way to appease her mammy would be by offering her a ringside seat at the next ultrasound appointment.

Nobody noticed Pooh had skulked off earlier. He'd slunk back into the room with his number one go-to toy. Donal's flip-flop. Nor did any of them spot Kiera drop the biscuit as she made a beeline for Pooh because Moira's voice was echoing down the hall. 'Mammy! Rosi's after ringing me to say Aisling and Quinn are having twins. Would you believe it?'

She strode into the room in time to see her chocolate-covered daughter engaged in a tug-o-war with Pooh over Donal's flip-flop.

'Jaysus wept. Mammy, what's going on?' Moira demanded, coming up short, hands on hips.

At the sound of her mammy's voice, Kiera dropped the flip-flop and crawled with surprising speed towards her shouting, 'Ma, ma, ma!'

'She goes like the clappers,' Quinn said, watching in amazement as she paused by the Christmas tree, having decided to snatch and grab the silver bauble. He swept her up in the nick of time and presented her to her mother.

'She's legs made for the Irish dancing, alright,' Maureen said. 'You watch she'll be a world champion. Donal, would you ring Louise about that guardrail you were after mentioning she had when her children were small?'

'I will, Mo.' Donal chortled and added, 'And to think there'll be two more getting about the place before we know it.'

Aisling burst into tears once more.

Chapter Seven

♥

Aisling waved the offer of a second cup of tea away and turned her nose up at the chocolate ginger biscuit. 'I'm alright, Mammy. Stop fussing. It's my hormones.' She was suddenly exhausted and wanted nothing more than to crawl into bed and close her eyes. That wasn't going to happen, though. They still had to call in on the Morans before they went home.

Quinn had a protective arm wrapped around his wife's shoulders. 'It's the hormones,' he repeated with the wariness of a man used to tiptoeing around them.

Aisling watched Moira clean her squirming daughter's face. Who would have believed that two years earlier, her sister was the glossy, party girl about town? Aisling thought she'd come a long way, noticing she looked every inch the art student today in her boho-chic attire. She took after Mammy in that respect with her need to look the part, and it wouldn't surprise her if her sister started stomping about in Dr Martens next. Still, the bonus was she wasn't sneaking out the door with her favourite Louboutin's anymore. Well, not as much as she used to, at any rate.

A sudden growling over by the French doors started up, and heads swivelled in that direction to see Donal engaged in a fierce tug-of-war for the flip-flop with Pooh.

Pooh bared his pointy poodly teeth, and Donal let go. He'd been on the receiving end of those before and had no wish to repeat the experience. Pooh was victorious, flopping down on the mat and wrapping his paws protectively over the flip-flop. A defeated Donal took himself off to the kitchen to ring Louise about the guardrail.

'Mammy, I need a cup of tea for the shock like,' Moira piped up, patting Kiera's bottom to see if she needed a nappy change while she was at it.

'It's not you who's having the twins, and are your hands painted on?'

'Sure, I've a child to be tending to, Mammy. A child whose baby teeth are at risk of rotting thanks to all the chocolate her nana feeds her when I'm not around. Not to mention a child at risk of contracting a fungi mouth.'

Maureen slunk off to make the tea.

'I can't believe it.' Moira turned her attention to Aisling as she sat back on her heels, keeping a tight hold of Kiera, who was reaching pudgy arms out towards the Christmas tree. 'Twins.' She shook her head, and her dark hair shimmered under the light.

'Have you been using my salon-only shampoo?' Aisling demanded. 'It's expensive, and you don't need the extra body. Sure, you've loads of it.' She picked up a lank strawberry-blonde lock and gave it a desultory glance.

'I haven't touched your shampoo,' Moira fibbed, not looking at her sister as she wrested the changing mat from the baby bag and pinned Kiera to it. 'Pass me a nappy, would you, please, Quinn.'

He did so, smiling as Moira repeated herself. 'I can't believe you're having twins.' She deftly whipped Kiera's nappy off and went through the changing routine.

'Neither can we,' Quinn replied for them both.

'I mean twins.'

'I heard you the first time, Moira,' Aisling snapped.

'Yeah, but—'

'Mammy! Tell her I'll scream if she says twins one more time.'

'Moira, stop winding your sister up when she's with...' Maureen frowned, a cup of tea in hand as she tried to work out the plural of with child, 'babbies.' She placed Moira's drink down on the side table. 'Keep an eye on Kiera with that.'

Moira pulled her daughter's corduroy trousers back up and let her go before sitting next to her sister and taking a greedy gulp of her tea. 'Ah, that's better. And it's grand news, so it is, Ash. Tom will be thrilled for you both too.' She did an excited jiggle, nearly sloshing her tea. 'Kiera's going to have two new babby cousins to boss about.' Then she took Aisling by surprise by reaching out and squeezing her hand. 'And I'll be about, to show you the ropes if that's what's got you bursting into tears.'

Tears threatened once more at Moira's uncharacteristic kindness and Aisling blinked rapidly. 'Thanks, Moira, but you're still not allowed to use my Wella Balsam.'

Quinn had taken over the brick tower building, and Kiera was rocking with excitement as she waited for him to finish so she could knock it down once more when Maureen reappeared. This time she had the telephone in her hand. 'How's about we ring Patrick now we're all together?'

Aisling was about to say, Do we have to? but Maureen was already speed-dialling her firstborn. So far as Aisling was concerned, her brother was one of life's takers. A chancer, but when he'd borrowed money off Mammy with no attempts having been made to pay it back, he'd gone a step too far, in her opinion.

'Hello there, Cindy,' Maureen said a few seconds later, putting her on speaker phone in time for the sisters to grin as their brother's girlfriend replied, 'Mom!' in her breathy Marilyn Monroe voice.

Maureen blanched as she was apt to do at this term of endearment from her son's live-in girlfriend, but nothing was going to take the shine off this moment. 'I'm after ringing from Dublin with some exciting news. Is Patrick about?'

'I think she knows you're not ringing from Istanbul, Mammy,' Moira muttered, causing Aisling to snigger.

'Mom, that is just the funniest thing! Would you believe Pat and I were about to ring you with some exciting news? He's on the balcony closing a deal. I'll tell him you're on the phone.'

They heard her call out, 'Pat, Mom's on the phone from Dublin!'

Maureen looked like she was developing a tic hearing all those 'moms'. She'd no intention of divulging the exciting news until Patrick came on the line, and her mind whirred, wondering what it was her son and his girlfriend had to share. 'Have you plenty of work on at the moment, Cindy?' she asked.

'Mom, I'm in demand. Word's spread ever since the feminine wipes advertisement. I've just got back from filming a commercial this morning.'

'That's grand, that is,' Maureen said, hoping to head her off there.

'It was for Easy, Breezy Tampons.'

'Very good,' Maureen said.

'I was a ballerina who does a pirouette and then the splits before holding the tampon box out to the camera and saying my lines. "Dancing's easy with Easy Breezy",' Cindy cooed.

At a loss for words, Maureen glared at Aisling and Moira. The sisters were in fits picturing their brother's top-heavy girlfriend in a tutu with a packet of tampons in her hand.

'How're you, Mammy?' Patrick's voice boomed out, saving Maureen from having to reply.

She glowed hearing her firstborn and only son's voice. 'Very well, Patrick. I'm after getting some special shoes made which will help with my knees. Are you eating enough?' She disapproved of the fad diets Cindy always seemed to have them both on.

'I am, Mammy. Cindy told you we have something to tell you?'

'She did, and we've something to tell you at our end too. But you first, son.' Maureen locked eyes with her daughters and mouthed, 'I'll swing for the pair of yer'. They settled down, curious to hear Patrick and Cindy's news.

'You tell them,' Cindy said, giggling.

'No, you,' Patrick said.

'You're so sweet.' An indecipherable sound followed.

'I think they're snogging,' Moira whispered before pretending to gag.

'Patrick, this is an international phone call, son. The pennies are stacking up,' Maureen informed him.

There was giggling and scuffling, and then Cindy came on the line. 'Sorry, Mom. Guess what? Patrick asked me to marry him, and I said yes! So I'm officially going to be Mrs Cindy O'Mara! Your daughter.' Her squeal saw them collectively wince. Kiera began crying.

'Mammy, did you hear what Cindy said?' Patrick demanded as the only sound in the Howth living room was Kiera howling.

'Mammy, say something.' Moira nudged her before getting down on the floor to tend to her daughter.

'Donal, would you fetch Mammy a glass of water. She's after turning a funny colour?' Aisling asked.

He was already on to it.

'It's two big surprises in one day that's done it,' Donal said, returning with a glass. 'Have a sip, Maureen.'

'I think it's something stronger than water she's needing,' Quinn said.

Aisling prised the telephone from her mammy's fingers. 'Hello there, Pat, Cindy. It's Aisling. Mammy's crying with happiness, so she is. You'd not get a coherent word from her.

So I'm saying congratulations to you both on her and our behalf. Welcome to the family, Cindy.'

'Thank you!' In her excitement, Cindy carried on at a hundred miles an hour. 'Pat and I are thinking of the Greek Islands or maybe Hawaii. A beach wedding. I want you, Moira, Rosi and my sister Sherry to be bridesmaids!'

Jaysus! Aisling hoped she wasn't planning a Pam and Tommy-Lee swimsuit-style wedding. 'That's lovely, Cindy, thank you, but I've some news that might put a spanner in the works where Quinn and I are concerned. We went for our three-month scan this morning and discovered we're having twins.'

There was another squeal that set Kiera off wailing once more. 'Oh my God, that's fantastic, sis!'

Sis? Aisling blinked. She was in danger of joining Mammy in her catatonic state.

Patrick gave a gruff congratulations. However, Maureen's trance broke at the mention of a beach wedding, and she snatched the phone back off Aisling. 'What's all this about Hawaii and the Greek Islands? Sure, what's wrong with getting married in Dublin? Haven't we got St Stephen's Green for the wedding photos? The lake with the ducks all swimming about comes up a treat in the photographs, so it does.'

Aisling and Moira exchanged a glance that said the Dublin summer was not one to hedge your bets on if you wanted an outdoor wedding. But Mammy seemed to be missing the point, and she wasn't finished yet either.

'Or there's a grand church right here in Howth. You could have a lovely reception in the hall and have your photos taken on the pier.'

'But, Mom, we want to get married on the beach with the sand between our toes. So we're thinking next summer.'

'You'll be hard-pressed to find a priest willing to get sand in his papal slippers, Cindy. Besides, he'd cook in his vestments in the elements like so.'

'But, Mom, we won't be having a priest. Will we, Patrick?

Aisling could picture Patrick squirming next to his fiancée. Fecky brown-noser, wimp.

'Patrick, what's Cindy talking about?'

'Uh, Mammy, the thing is, well, what Cindy and I would like—'

It was clear who would be wearing the underpants in their marriage, Aisling thought as Cindy took charge. 'What Pat's trying to tell you, Mom, is a good friend of ours, Bobby-Jean, is a celebrant, and she'll be marrying us.

Donal appeared with a tumbler with a splash of amber liquid in it.

He was a good man, was Donal, Maureen thought, knocking it back.

Chapter Eight

A cross town, Freya hurried through St Stephen's Green. Her face was barely visible between the woolly hat pulled low over her ears and the collar of the coat she was hunched inside. Her socks were damp, thanks to the puddle she'd inadvertently stepped in, and the strap on her backpack was digging into her shoulder. She readjusted it with a grimace. The pack was heavy, thanks to the books she needed for the course she'd begun in September at the Dublin Institute of Technology.

It was a conversation with her Great Aunt Nono that had planted the seed for broadening her horizons with a hospitality management course. Freya had been dropping hints to her about how she'd love to travel and see more of the world. The farthest she'd been was Curracloe in County Wexford on a camping holiday when she was twelve.

Freya knew her great aunt was a generous woman who thought of Freya's mam, Emer as a daughter. Sure they even lived together in Claredoncally. So theoretically, that made her a granddaughter. It was tough to save, she'd explained, given what she earned on the shop floor of the Boots where she'd been working at the time. She had a room in a shared house too, which meant there were bills to fork out for. Admittedly, she'd been laying it on thick, but Great Aunt Nono was old and she wanted to be sure she understood what she was getting at. She hadn't.

Instead of offering to fund a holiday abroad like she had her mam when the pair of them had gone tripping off to Los Angeles a year or two ago, she'd mentioned Aisling O'Mara, who was a grand girl altogether. Freya knew the O'Mara family ran a Dublin guesthouse but had never been sure how they were related. Her doddery old aunt had gone on to say Aisling had led a glamourous life in her twenties flitting around the world managing holiday resorts. Then, when her father had passed away, she'd come home to take over running O'Mara's. Sure, why didn't Freya look into doing something down that line if she'd the itchy feet?

It had been remarked upon more than once in Freya's childhood that she'd do well to listen to others on occasion. And, for once in her life, she had.

Freya enrolled at the Dublin Institute of Technology and gave notice at work and on her flat before calling it a day with her boyfriend, Liam. None of which had been difficult. In Freya's opinion, given her extensive knowledge of the cosmetics she sold, she was underpaid, her flat was draughty, and her flatmates finicky. She'd known Liam wasn't a keeper because he had no ambition, unlike herself. As for saying goodbye to friends, there weren't many, which didn't bother her because she wasn't the sort of girl who needed lots of people around her.

She squinted at her watch in the gloom. It was only three forty-five in the afternoon, but it was already dark, not to mention freezing. The park smelled of wet leaves and wrinkling her nose at the sight of a smouldering butt, cigarettes. Freya hated winter. People were intent on getting to their destination with as little interaction as possible, whereas in summer, they'd meander to wherever they were going and greet you with a nod and a smile; point in proof, the woman about to pass by her. She was holding an umbrella as though it was a weapon and looked like she'd jab you with it if you dared offer any pleasantries.

As she neared the exit to the park, Freya daydreamed that one day she'd manage a swanky resort in the Maldives or perhaps Thailand. Somewhere hot, exotic and as far away from Ireland as possible. There was no one here she'd miss or who'd miss her. Her two siblings kept themselves to themselves; as for Mam, she'd always put herself first. She wasn't a natural mother in that respect, and when the going got tough for her, she'd been indignant when her children hadn't rallied around. That was when she'd latched on to Great Aunt Nono, who'd been lonely and grateful for the companionship.

Freya wasn't like her mam though. She wouldn't leech off others because she had a plan to forge her way to where she wanted to be.

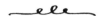

'Good afternoon, Mr Fortner.' Freya dimpled at their American guest. He was browsing the brochures as she closed the door to the guesthouse behind her. She was grateful to come in from the cold and, wiping her feet on the mat, saw he was looking at a flyer advertising Johnny Fox's. 'I can recommend Quinn's for dinner if you want an authentic Irish dining experience. The craic's mighty and the food's great. Even better, it's only five minutes down the road.' She'd never even been to Quinn's but had heard Aisling use this pitter-patter and had no qualms in doling it out herself.

'Thank you, Freya.' Mr Fortner, who had an impressively slow drawl hailing from the southern USA as he did, smiled back at her. He unconsciously stood a little straighter, pleased she'd remembered his name given their only prior encounter was when he and his wife had ventured out to a show the night before.

Freya whipped her woolly hat off. She could feel the static and quickly smoothed her hair.

Bronagh put the phone down and finished scribbling down the message she was taking. Then she pushed up from her seat to greet their night receptionist. 'How're you, Freya? A good day at college, was it?'

'It was very interesting, Bronagh. We were learning all about hospitality law today.'

Bronagh's eyes had glazed over at the mention of law. The only law she was interested in was your Ally McBeal wan on the television. There was a time when she'd worn skirts as short as Ally's, before the menopause, of course. She nodded at Freya nonetheless, wanting to encourage the young woman in her chosen career. 'That's grand, that is,' she said, slipping into her coat, ready for the off because she planned on catching Cherry on Top before they closed. The cake shop's hummingbird speciality was calling her, and she hoped they hadn't sold out. It was Wednesday, and she usually ducked out at lunchtime to ensure she managed to get two wedges of what took her fancy, but with Aisling out for the day, there'd been no opportunity to do so.

Bronagh had settled into a comfortable routine of calling in on Lennie's sister Joan with a cardboard box from Cherry on Top in her hands after work on Wednesdays. They'd sip their tea, fork up their cake and put the world to rights. It was most enjoyable. She'd never met a woman with a sweet tooth to match her own. Aisling ran close, but she and Joan were soul sisters regarding all things cake. 'I'm in a rush tonight, Freya,' she said, picking up her handbag. 'There are some reservations that need to be loaded in the basket, and if you could be sure to pass on the message, I've just jotted down for Sara Scott in Room 5 when she comes back in. That's most important.'

'Will do. I'll see you tomorrow, Bronagh. Enjoy your evening.'

She was such a pleasant young woman, Bronagh thought and saying, 'See you tomorrow,' she hurried out of the door, pausing only to wish Mr Fortner a good evening.

Their American guest's wife descended the stairs as Freya made her way towards the small kitchenette where she could hang her things up and heat the frozen dinner she'd picked up later. 'Good evening, Mrs Fortner.' She blinked, blinded by the baubles she had dripping off her. Over the top seemed to be the woman's standard attire, and she looked like she should be dining at the captain's table on the *QE2* ocean liner. Freya didn't know much about the Southern States of America, but she had heard of debutantes, and she'd happily bet on Mrs Fortner having worn a fancy dress with white gloves for her debut. 'You're looking lovely tonight.'

'Thank you, dear. Mr Fortner and I thought we might venture out for a pre-dinner cocktail.'

'Oh, have you booked somewhere for dinner?'

'No. We were toying with the Shelbourne.'

'Clementine, have a look at this.' Mr Fortner called his wife over, and Freya saw he had the brochure for Quinn's in his hand.

She quickly stepped into the kitchenette, dumped her bag, hung up her coat, and shoved the 99p Iceland prawn curry in the fridge before venturing back to reception. The couple were examining the menu.

It's the personal touch, Freya, she told herself, brushing the lint off her trousers and tucking in her blouse at the back before donning her professional persona. 'Quinn's is very popular, Mr and Mrs Fortner,' she said, a note of regret in her voice. 'Our guests love the craic that's to be had there.'

'Oh.' Mrs Fortner's shoulder pads slumped. 'Should we have made a reservation? Truman, I told you we should have booked ahead for dinner. It looks fun, and I have a hankering for that there, coddle.' She prodded the brochure.

Freya knew they were checking out and flying home to Georgia the next day. 'Listen, Quinn's is usually a full house, but as you're valued guests of ours here at O'Mara's, why don't you let me give them a call and see what I can do?'

'Would you mind?'

'That would be wonderful.'

Mrs Fortner clasped her hands, and Mr Fortner jingled the coins in his pocket.

Freya telephoned the bistro, hopeful she'd be able to book a table for two, given it was Wednesday. It rang four times before their maître d, Alasdair answered. 'Hello, Alasdair, it's Freya from O'Mara's here.' There was a pause. 'Very well, thank you. Now, I know it's short notice, but would it be possible to find a table for two special guests of ours?' She held up a pair of crossed fingers and Mrs Fortner did the same back at her. It was amusing how desperate they now were to dine at Quinn's, given they'd not heard of it until Freya had steered Mr Fortner in that direction.

'You can?' She gave a thumbs-up before putting her hand over the receiver. 'Would seven pm work?'

The Fortners' necks were in danger of dislocating, so enthusiastically did they nod.

'Freya, you've made us as happy as a couple of clams at high tide. You're a peach, and I'll be sure to tell your manager about the wonderful service you've given us.'

'And here's a little something for your trouble,' Mr Fortner said, pulling a wad of notes from his wallet and pressing them towards Freya.

'Oh no, Mr Fortner. There's no need for that. I was happy to help. And I'm so pleased you'll get to experience Dublin's finest food and music before you leave.'

'I insist. It's our way, and I'll be offended if you don't accept, won't I, Clementine?'

'He will,' Clementine agreed.

'Well, I've no wish to offend you.' Freya smiled and took the money, feeling a little thrill seeing the zeroes. 'That's very generous of you. Thanks a million. You be sure to enjoy the craic tonight.'

'I just love your cute little Irishisms.' Clementine smiled, linking her arm through her husband's. 'Now, I do believe there's a gin fizz with my name on it at the Shelbourne. Shall we, Truman?'

'Allow me, my dear.'

Freya watched them go, feeling pleased with herself as she pocketed the notes. Tips were supposed to be shared between the staff, something Freya disagreed with. She'd earned that money fair and square, so why should she share it?

Her eyes strayed to the message Bronagh had asked her to pass on to Sara Scott when she returned to the guesthouse. Aisling had told her that Sara Scott's wish was to be her command while she was staying at O'Mara's, given she suspected she was an undercover hotel inspector.

A smile played at the corners of Freya's mouth as she plucked the message off the spike and, screwing it up, shoved it in the pocket of her trousers. It was terrible how forgetful Bronagh was getting. She was becoming a liability, she thought, smirking.

Chapter Nine

♥

W hat would she call them? Aisling wondered. She'd had a jelly bean for the last three months, and now she had two. Jelly beans? Why not? Pleased she'd come up with a solution, Aisling stretched out further on the sofa and waggled her feet at Moira squashed into the corner down the other end. Tom was banging about in the kitchen, putting together his speciality, meat and three veg. He was fond of saying it wasn't exciting but was nutritional.

Aisling had preferred it when his go-to was spag bog. He had a night off from waiting tables at Quinn's and had been keen to cook. Kiera had been tucked into her cot fifteen minutes earlier, and after her busy day at Nana and Poppa D's, she'd gone out like a light.

'Stop it,' Moira growled in the direction of the feet.

'Please, it will take my mind off feeling sick.' The smell of the cabbage Tom was boiling to death was turning Aisling's stomach. It wasn't an aroma to entice you to the dinner table in the first place, but her sense of smell had become super sensitive of late, and it was enough to make her gag. She'd already decided to fine dine on the bone broth Quinn had made her with dry toast and a gingernut for dessert. It was too bad he was at the restaurant because he could be counted on for foot rubbing.

'Get them out of my face.' Moira looked a little demented now as she began to bat at her sister's feet as though trying to swat an enormous mosquito.

'You owe me, Moira.' Wiggle waggle went the toes that needed a pedicure. Aisling, who was ordinarily fastidious about her feet given her love of designer shoes, had not had the energy to attend to this. Unpainted toenails inside Jimmy Choo's were like wearing knickers that had been washed so many times they'd gone grey and lost their shape under a Dior gown. That she'd allowed hers to get into their current state attested to how unwell she'd been feeling for the last three months. 'Shampoo, shampoo, shampoo,' she chanted, desperate to get her way.

'I didn't touch your Wella Balsam, or whatever that yoke in the shower is,' Moira said, pushing her extremely lustrous locks back from her shoulders, 'And I'm trying to watch this.' She pretended she was engrossed in the Palestinian and Israeli situation the journalist on the television was informing them about.

'Since when do you have any interest in the world around you?'

'Children change you, Aisling,' Moira replied loftily. 'You'll see.'

'Feck off away with yer. Not that much they don't because you still pinch my shampoo and shoes.' Aisling's stomach rolled as Tom began to fry the chops, and she groaned.

'I do not. And I can't hear you anyway.' Moira cranked the volume up.

'Moira, pretty please with sugar on top.'

Moira turned to her sister, looking past her feet to her pasty face. 'Will you name one of the twins after me if you have a girl and Tom if you have a boy?'

'No.'

'Then it's a no to the foot rub.' She went back to the news. It wasn't true what Aisling had said about her having no interest in the world around her because she was very interested in finding out what shade of blush the presenter wore. That shade of pink would look well on her, she decided.

Aisling was about to protest again when the telephone rang, and Tom abandoned his post to answer it. He looked towards Aisling, 'For you,' he said, crossing the room to pass it to her. Moira turned the volume down on the television.

'Thanks, Tom.' She eyed the phone in her hand, hoping it wasn't Mammy ringing to harp on about Patrick and Cindy's proposed al fresco wedding. She'd heard enough that afternoon, but as she pressed it to her ear and said hello, she was surprised to hear Freya's voice.

'Aisling, I'm sorry to bother you, but we have a situation with Sara Scott. Would you be able to come down to reception because I want your okay with how I plan on resolving it?'

Sara Scott had thundered down to reception five minutes earlier, demanding to know why the message her colleague had left asking her to book a table for two at The Clarence hadn't been passed on when she'd returned to the guesthouse earlier. Her face was mottled an angry red as she said it was too late to secure a table anywhere half decent now.

Freya had been effusive in her apology for Bronagh's oversight in not taking the message down before asking the woman, who was only a couple of years older than herself, to leave it with her. The guest had thumped back up the stairs, and Freya had picked up the phone to telephone Aisling upstairs.

Oh no! Aisling thought, hauling herself upright. What had happened? And to Sara Scott of all people. There was no point in trying to find out over the phone. 'I'll be down in two ticks.' To her surprise, she felt better sitting up and, slipping her socks back on, slid her feet into her abandoned Manolo Blahnik's underneath the coffee table.

'What's going on?' Moira asked, already swivelling so she could stretch out on the sofa.

'Freya said there's a situation with a guest, and not just any guest, the woman I'm ninety-nine point nine per cent certain is a hotel inspector.'

'A situation? Who does she think she is, Tony Soprano?'

Aisling ignored her sister. Moira wasn't a fan of Freya's because of who her mother was. None of them knew what it was Emer had done. They only knew something had happened between her and Great Aunt Noreen years ago. Whatever it was, it was water under the bridge these days because Emer had attached herself leech-like to her comfortably off aunt. Aisling had told Moira she'd initially had the same worries about Freya, but her concerns were proving unfounded. It was an unfair presumption because the same could be said of them where their mammy was concerned, she'd added before asking, 'Do we have a soft spot for Daniel Day-Lewis in his loin cloth, listen to country music and do the line dancing? No, we do not.'

Moira had retorted, 'That's different, and Mammy hasn't watched *Last of the Mohicans* since she met Donal. You wait, Ash, Freya will show her true colours before long.' She'd also said she was a better judge of character than Aisling, to which she received the response, 'You're delusional.'

Moira took stock of her sister's pale face and lank hair and felt guilty. Not for pinching her shampoo mind but because she did look worn out. 'Let me go and see what the problem is.'

'You will not. You've got as much tact as Pooh when he wants his dinner. I don't want O'Mara's getting a bad rating in the triple-A travel guide. I'll sort it myself.' She didn't mean to be short. Moira was only trying to help, she thought, standing up. 'Sorry, I didn't mean to snap.'

'I'll forgive you if you let the shampoo thing go.'

'Fine,' Aisling said, leaving her sister and Tom to get their dinner sorted. The familiar scent of furniture polish from the banister rails Ita had polished to a high sheen that day was a welcome respite from Tom's overboiled cabbage and chops, she thought, haring down the stairs. She hoped whatever had happened with Sara Scott was salvageable.

'Good evening,' she called out, barely pausing to wave at the Bagshaws. They were dressed in their best bibs and tuckers, but Aisling didn't have time to stop and ask them where they were off to. Instead, she hurried down the final flight of stairs to the foyer and was only three steps from the bottom when her heel snagged on the carpet. Her arms windmilled out either side, and she swayed forwards and then backwards before landing in a heap on the floor.

Freya, hearing Aisling's cry shot out from behind her desk where she'd been eagerly anticipating saving the day, or evening as it were, where Sara Scott was concerned.

'Aisling?' She dropped down to where her employer was crumpled at the foot of the stairs, her face hidden by a curtain of reddish, blonde hair. 'Aisling.' Her voice was urgent. She vaguely registered the Bagshaws had appeared on the landing above.

'I'm a nurse,' Mrs Bagshaw said, making her way down the stairs, and Freya moved aside, relieved to let the older woman take charge watching as Mrs Bagshaw brushed Aisling's hair back, revealing her ashen face.

'My babies,' Aisling whispered.

Chapter Ten

♥

A isling sat on the sofa in reception. The sweetened cup of tea Freya had fetched her from the guests' lounge and from which she'd had a tentative few sips was on the coffee table. She'd also put two custard creams on the saucer, pilfered from Bronagh's biscuit stash, but under the circumstances, she was sure the receptionist wouldn't mind. The cup had rattled as Aisling placed it back in its saucer, sending tea slopping over the side, but her shaking began to subside once the sugar hit her system. The now soggy biscuits were still on the side of the saucer.

Freya watched Mrs Bagshaw, grateful to her for stepping in. She and her husband had helped Aisling, who'd hurt her ankle in the fall, upright, and as they settled her on the sofa, she'd raced off to make the tea. Still in shock, Aisling had been apologising for having ruined their evening.

'Nonsense. We're always far too early for everything. We've plenty of time to make the show, so don't you be worrying about us,' Mr Bagshaw reassured her, moving away from the sofa to stand near the brochures. He straightened his dicky bow looking uncomfortable as he fidgeted his hands in the pocket of his black suit trousers.

Freya, who'd decided she was best not hovering over Aisling, sat back down behind the reception desk and, taking the initiative, picked up the phone. Quinn needed to know what had happened, and tapping out the restaurant's number on the yellow Post-it beside the computer, she listened to it ring. Mrs Bagshaw was speaking in a cheery tone that managed to be simultaneously authoritative and comforting.

'Alright, then, Aisling, let's make sure everything is tickety-boo. I take it you're pregnant?'

'Three months. I'm having jelly beans. I mean twins.' Aisling's eyes were orbs, and her face was pale.

'Congratulations.' Mrs Bagshaw smiled, and Aisling managed a shaky one in return.

Freya's own eyes popped hearing this. Twins? That was a turn-up. She straightened the pile of reservations Bronagh had left for her to enter into the Mac, fretfully hoping everything was alright. She'd gathered enough from snippets of conversation she'd overheard that the road to getting pregnant for Aisling hadn't been straightforward. Her employer had looked washed out these last few months, but her underlying excitement was clear. The phone rang for at least the eighth time, and she was about to hang up and try again when it was picked up by Quinn's effusive maître d, Alasdair. 'Hello, it's Freya Lynch from the reception of O'Mara's Guesthouse. May I speak to Quinn, please? It's urgent.' She took several gulps of air because there was no point in panicking Quinn by communicating her anxiety down the phone.

While Mrs Bagshaw checked Aisling over, Freya managed to convey what had happened calmy to Quinn, explaining that Aisling was in the care of a nurse who happened to be staying at the guesthouse and didn't appear to be seriously hurt. She left out the awful thudding and cry she'd heard and Aisling's sickly pallor when the Bagshaws had helped her to her feet. Quinn interrupted her as she asked whether he wanted to speak to Aisling, saying he'd come straight home. It took Freya a moment to realise he'd hung up. She wondered whether she should call upstairs and tell Moira what had happened, but then the memory of her last call asking Aisling to come down to reception saw her shift uncomfortably in her seat. It would be her fault if anything happened to those babies Aisling was carrying. She wished she could rewind time, but there was nothing she could do now except make things right with Sara Scott. It would involve side-stepping Aisling's approval, but needs must, and she made another call to Quinn's, speaking directly to Alasdair. He was eager to help.

'Our bodies are marvellous things,' Mrs Bagshaw was saying. 'Your little babies are well protected by the amniotic fluid and uterus wall lining, Aisling, but if you'd been near the end of your second trimester or into your third, things might be different. I don't think there's anything to worry about, but it wouldn't hurt to get checked over by your doctor tomorrow.' Then, seeing Aisling's stricken face at the mention of a doctor, Mrs Bagshaw quickly added, 'For your peace of mind more than anything. Now let's get your boots off and look at those ankles, shall we?'

Aisling nodded, thinking O'Mara's guest was the sort of nurse anyone would be lucky to have in their time of need, as she allowed the older woman to unzip and then ease her boots off. She had a no-nonsense manner that had stopped the blood thundering through Aisling's ears as her pulse began to settle.

The older woman gently rotated her patient's left sock-clad foot, watching Aisling's face. She winced when the off-duty nurse moved across to do the same to the right ankle, which was swelling.

'Hmm, you're going to have some nasty bruising, but it's not sprained or broken. Nothing a bag of frozen peas won't fix.' Mrs Bagshaw's gaze flitted to the spike-heeled Manolo Blahnik ankle boots, and she raised an eyebrow. 'You might want to rethink your footwear though.'

Aisling stared gratefully up at the coiffed woman who smelled of something French and expensive. 'Thank you,' she croaked. 'I will.' She would happily get around in her trainers from hereon in.

'The best thing you can do, and I mean this, Aisling.' Mrs Bagshaw adopted a stern tone. 'Is rest this evening, do you understand? Put your feet up, get ice on that ankle, and do nothing.'

'I do, and I will.'

'Aisling, would you like me to get Moira?' Freya had left her seat and lingered beside her desk, relieved at the prognosis.

She must have given her an awful fright tumbling down the stairs like so, Aisling thought. 'I'm sorry, Freya, Mr and Mrs Bagshaw. I feel like a complete eejit for having scared you all.'

'I think it was you who was scared the most. And I'm glad I was on hand,' Mrs Bagshaw said, straightening as her husband, who Aisling wasn't even aware had left reception, returned with a sparkling purse in hand. He passed it to his wife.

'You dropped it at the foot of the stairs.'

'So I did.'

'Well, I'm glad it's nothing more than a bruised ankle.' Freya spoke up. Aisling would never know just how glad.

'Me too. And sure, there's no need to get Moira. I'll be going up in a minute anyway. Would you ring a taxi for Mr and Mrs Bagshaw please, Freya? Our compliments.'

'Oh, no, there's no need, really,' Mr Bagshaw shook his head as Freya enquired where they were going. 'We'll help you back upstairs.'

'There's every need. It's the least I can do,' Aisling asserted. She felt stronger, knowing the jelly beans were safe despite the throbbing ankle. The only downside of living in a Georgian manor house was all the stairs, and she didn't relish the thought of climbing them, but the couple had done enough. 'Freya will help me. Won't you?'

'Of course I will.'

'That's settled. Where should Freya tell the taxi company you're off to?'

'If you're sure?'

'Absolutely sure.'

'Well, thank you.' Mr Bagshaw turned to look over at Freya. 'We're off to the Gaiety, thank you.'

'You're going to the opera?' Aisling asked, aware the Irish National Opera had a show on there because it was her job to know these things. She'd only been once, and opera wasn't her cup of tea, but she'd appreciated the beautiful costumes and soaring voices.

The couple nodded. 'We're opera buffs. Ever since we saw *Madam Butterfly* performed in Rome when we were on our honeymoon,' Mrs Bagshaw said, her gaze soft on her husband. 'And, I have to say we're rather starved of it in Sligo where we live. So when we saw *Tosca* was on in Dublin, we decided to treat ourselves to a city break.'

'How lovely. I hope you have a wonderful evening,' Aisling said.

'The taxi will be here in a few minutes,' Freya announced, then, leaving the trio chatting, decided it would be best to speak to their undercover guest in person. Nobody saw her disappear up the stairs.

Quinn burst through the door before the taxi arrived with a jacket thrown over the top of his chef's uniform. He was out of breath and red-faced. His denim eyes swept from Aisling to the couple in evening dress and back to Aisling.

'It's okay, Quinn, I'm okay.'

'She is, a swollen ankle for her sins, but apart from that, she'll be good as new after a rest,' Mrs Bagshaw assured him.

'Mrs Bagshaw here's a nurse, and it was lucky for me she was here when I fell.'

'Thank you for looking after her.' Quinn looked at her gratefully before turning to Aisling. 'Freya said you tripped on the stairs?'

'It sounds much worse than it was.' Looking at her husband's stricken face, Aisling wished Freya hadn't telephoned him, but at the same time, she was relieved to see him. She realised the front desk was deserted and wondered where Freya had gone before filling in the blanks for Quinn. 'I was halfway between the first-floor landing and the ground when my heel caught in the carpet.' Both their eyes strayed to the offending spike-heeled boots.

Aisling had been wearing heels forever. She could jog in the things if she had to and skipped up and down the stairs at O'Mara's daily. Okay, so jog and skip were gross exaggerations. The point was she was as comfortable in a pair of stilettos as she was in her stockinged feet. Yet, tonight she'd taken a tumble that could have seen her lose their precious babies. 'I promise I won't be wearing anything higher than my trainers from here on in.'

'Good.' Quinn sank down next to her on the sofa tugging off his jacket before undoing the first few poppers on his chef's jacket. 'I ran here,' he said, which explained his heavy breathing.

A toot sounded outside.

'That will be your taxi,' Aisling said to the couple before thanking them again for their help. She made a note to herself to take the new Dublin tour company, touting for business, up on their offer of a complimentary day trip encompassing Glendalough and Powerscourt Estate as a thank you to the couple for taking care of her.

'Yes, thanks so much,' Quinn echoed, repeating his earlier sentiment as the Bagshaws took their leave. He grasped hold of Aisling's hand. 'Come on, let's get you upstairs.'

Aisling let him help her to her feet, following his instructions to lean on him, so she didn't put weight on her right ankle. They'd got as far as the foot of the stairs when Freya appeared on the landing above them. Her face was flushed, and Aisling remembered what it was that had brought her downstairs in the first place. Sara Scott. She tried to read their night receptionist's expression as she descended, but it was a closed book unlike hers.

'Everything's grand, Aisling. You're not to be worrying,' Freya said, interpreting her employer's frown correctly.

'Not to be worrying about what?' Quinn asked.

'A guest.' Freya directed this at Quinn. 'But everything is sorted out.'

Quinn nodded. 'Thanks for ringing me.' He looked at Aisling and then back at Freya. 'If this one had had her way, she'd have said nothing until I got in from work later.'

'Because I'm okay.' Aisling defended herself.

'I thought you'd want to know what had happened,' Freya said with a small smile. She liked Quinn. He was nice, and he looked like Ronan Keating.

'Would you mind giving us a hand?' he asked.

'Of course not.'

Aisling put her arm around Freya's shoulder and then they began the slow climb to the family apartment.

Freya smiled as they passed the second floor, where Sara Scott was getting ready to go out. Their guest's good humour was restored thanks to a complimentary meal at Quinn's Bistro for her and her friend this evening. Alasdair had promised Freya he'd be sure they were made to feel special.

Feeling Aisling leaning heavily on her, the fear that she was ultimately responsible for Aisling's fall floated away because she'd managed to fix everything. In a day or two, Aisling's ankle would be fine. Then, envisaging the pat on the back sure to come her way for how she'd handled their undercover inspector, she decided it would be worth having screwed Bronagh's message up. All that was left to do was figure out how to drop Bronagh's oversight into the conversation.

But that could wait for another day.

Chapter Eleven

♥

A isling lay on the sofa propped up by pillows with a blanket tossed over her. A packet of frozen peas wrapped in a tea towel rested on her ankle, and she was gnawing on a gingernut. The only bonus of having hurt her ankle was it had taken her mind off her earlier nausea. Her free hand rested protectively across her middle.

Tom had got extra GP practise in by running the same questions Mrs Bagshaw had asked earlier past her, and Doctor Tom was now sitting in the armchair watching an episode of *Emmerdale Farm*. For someone who claimed he'd no interest in the soap, he was engrossed in whatever drama was happening on the screen at the Woolpack Pub right now, Aisling thought. It didn't matter what was going on in your life. You could guarantee someone on *Emmerdale*, *Eastenders* or *Coronation Street* was having a worse time. They were a comforting thing, the British soaps, she mused.

Quinn had seemed satisfied by Tom's prognosis, the same as Mrs Bagshaw's, that the babies would be fine and that a bag of frozen veg along with rest would sort the ankle. Still, he kept darting concerned glances in her direction from where he was sitting on the carpet with his back resting against the sofa.

It was sweet, Aisling thought, reaching forward to ruffle his hair as she reassured him for the umpteenth time that everything was okay. It was also beginning to get a little annoying. She felt bad enough about what had happened and knew he was torturing himself with 'what if' scenarios. She wished he'd gone back to the restaurant to finish the night out, but he'd refused, and after telephoning to ensure the dinner service was running smoothly without him, he'd taken up his position on the floor by her side. Yawning, she thought she might take herself off to bed shortly. The evening's events had wiped her out.

'At least you won't be pestering me for a foot rub for the next few days,' Moira called from where she was loitering with the phone in the kitchen.

'Who're you after ringing?' Aisling was suddenly awake, and her eyes narrowed as she glared at her sister because she had a pretty good idea whose number she'd speed dialled.

'No one.' Moira tucked her dark hair behind her ears, turning away as she said, 'How're you, Mammy? Listen, Aisling's after falling down the stairs.'

She had the foresight to hold the phone away from her ears, and Aisling grimaced, hearing her mammy's shriek emanate from it.

It had been a day of shrieking, what with finding out they were having twins and Patrick and Cindy getting engaged. Now, this. 'Thanks a million, Moira. Put her on to me.' The last thing she needed was Mammy and Donal doing a mercy dash over from Howth. Mammy, with her 'Soldier-On' song, was not a natural nurse. Quinn holding vigil next to the sofa was bad enough. Moira placed the phone in her hand and Aisling, pressing it to her ear, said, 'The babies and myself are alright, Mammy.'

'Aisling, is that you?' Maureen had a white-knuckled grip on the phone at her end.

Aisling frowned. Who did Mammy think was on the phone? Some random pregnant woman hanging out in the family apartment? She bit the inside of her cheek to stop a smart remark from escaping. It wouldn't help.

Donal was also watching *Emmerdale*, but he pulled his attention from the television at the panicked sound of his live-in-lady friend's voice. 'She's had a fall down the stairs,' Maureen lobbed across the room at him.

Now poor Donal was getting dragged into the drama too. 'It was only a little tumble I was after taking. It's not a big deal—' Too late, Aisling realised that was the wrong thing to say.

'Not a big deal!' Maureen exploded. 'Aisling O'Mara, did I hear you right?'

'O'Mara-Moran, Mammy and all I said was it was only a little tumble.'

'You are with babbies. Not just any babbies. My grand-babbies. And you've fallen down the stairs thanks to those ridiculous heels you insist on gadding about in. Well, no more. Do you hear me?'

There wasn't much Aisling could say to that because it was true. Besides, she knew better than to interrupt her mammy mid-rant. 'I hear you, Mammy.'

'Good. It's the special shoes for you from now on.'

'Ah no, Mammy, not the special shoes. Sure, I've a pair of trainers I can wear. They'll be grand, so they will.'

'Aisling, it's not up for discussion. We'll pay Cathal Carrick a visit as soon as you're right. We can pick up my new boots while we're at it.' Maureen moved swiftly on before her daughter could protest further. 'Now, will you be needing to borrow my crutches? Because Donal and myself can be there in half an hour with them.'

'No. Sure, Mammy, I can put weight on my ankle. It's just bruised.'

'Put Quinn on, would you? I want to hear everything's alright from him.'

'Quinn, Mammy wants a word.' Aisling mouthed 'sorry' as she passed the phone to her husband.

'Aisling's fine, Maureen. I promise. She's been checked over by a guest who's a nurse, and Tom's satisfied everything is okay too.' Quinn was quiet for a second. Then he held the phone out towards Tom. 'Maureen wants a word with you, Tom.'

Tom didn't look away from whatever exciting events were unfolding in the Woolpack.

'Tom,' Quinn said louder, and Tom dragged his eyes away from the television. 'Maureen's on the phone wanting to know Aisling and the babies are alright. Would you tell her?'

Tom gazed longingly at the screen, thinking it was his night off and Kiera was asleep. So was it too much to ask to enjoy half an hour of television in peace? Knowing the answer was yes, he got up and took the phone.

'It's like pass the parcel only with the phone,' Moira said, shaking her head from where she was leaning on the worktop watching the proceedings.

'You're the one who rang her.' Aisling shot daggers over her shoulder before crunching into the remainder of her biscuit.

'It's alright for you, all sanctimonious over there on the sofa with your peas. Mammy would give me what for if I didn't ring her and she found out after the event.'

True, Aisling thought, slumping back against the pillows. 'Well, you don't need to ring Rosi if that's who you're thinking of phoning next.'

'Already have. But once Rosi heard you and the babies were okay, she started on about the gerbils and what a good little mammy Steve is. I hung up in the end. But I know, Rosi, and it's a pet babby gerbil for Kiera she's angling at. We can't take one because the poor thing wouldn't stand a chance. Kiera would have it in her mouth the moment we turned our backs. And you want to watch it, or she'll be after giving Moira and Tom Junior pet gerbils as christening gifts.'

'Moira! Don't be calling the twins Moira and Tom Junior,' Aisling bellowed. She'd felt lovely and relaxed there on the sofa until Moira had rung not only Mammy but Rosi too. Now her blood pressure was soaring.

Tom passed the phone back to Aisling. 'Maureen says you're not to be fighting with your sister because getting wound up is bad for the babbies.'

Don't shoot the messenger, Aisling, she told herself. Then, taking the phone from him snapped, 'Tell her to stop winding me up then, Mammy. And ring Rosi while you're at it and tell her we don't want any fecking baby gerbils.'

'I think you're in shock carrying on like so, Aisling. Listen to me now. Donal's already putting his jacket on.'

'No, Mammy. Quinn's here. Tom and Moira are here. You and Donal stay where you are!'

'Aisling, what was I just saying about it not being good for you to get het up?'

'Give me strength,' Aisling said through gritted teeth. 'Listen, Mammy, Mrs Bagshaw, the nurse said I need to rest, and so did Tom. So, I'm going to bed now, which means you and Donal would have a wasted trip, and I promise I'll book in to see Doctor Kinsella in the morning.'

'A third opinion never hurts, Aisling,' Maureen said, waving for Donal to stand down. 'You're to phone me after you've been to see Maggie tomorrow.'

The tension went out of Aisling's shoulders. 'I will, Mammy, straight after.'

'I'll say goodnight then.'

'G'night, Mammy.'

Chapter Twelve

♥

'Congratulations, you two! The results of your ultrasound were faxed through this morning.' Doctor Kinsella enthused. She was wearing her customary white coat over her civvies as she held the door to her room open for them. 'Twins! How exciting for you both.'

Aisling spotted the sensible heel on Maggie Kinsella's boots and wondered if she was destined to go through the rest of her life noticing other people's footwear, given she'd no choice but to wear flats. Lifting her eyes from the boots, she smiled at her doctor's effusive greeting, as did Quinn. It was an effort though because they'd both had a sleepless night.

They were lucky to have been slotted in. The worry in Quinn's voice had been palpable when he'd rung the surgery first thing, and even though it meant Dr Kinsella's appointments would run behind for the rest of the day, Geraldine on reception had fitted them in as early as she could. Aisling fancied it was because she'd rather deal with Quinn than have Maureen O'Mara on the telephone demanding an urgent appointment for her pregnant daughter!

The GP ushered them over to the two seats in front of her cluttered desk before closing the door behind them.

Aisling eyed the chair Doctor Kinsella was lowering herself into. It was one of those that swivelled all over the place on wheels. She hoped the good doctor didn't find herself flying out that window behind her one of these days when she flopped down in it. It was practical for her to be able to talk to her patients and then spin around to tap notes into the computer, she supposed.

'So, Aisling, I understand you had a fall last night. Is that right?'

Aisling nodded, her nails digging into her palms. The word 'fall' when it was said like so sounded dreadful. It conjured up images in her mind of elderly people breaking a hip or worse. She preferred to think of it as a little tumble no more, which was what she said. 'I took a little tumble down the stairs at O'Mara's. Three stairs, to be exact.'

Doctor Kinsella picked up her black-rimmed reading glasses that reminded Aisling of the shorter *Two Ronnies'* character Mammy had been on about the other day. She put them on and steepled her hands in front of her with her elbows resting on the desk listening to Aisling's explanation.

Quinn's hand sought out Aisling's, and his fingers entwined with hers as, once his wife's mouth had clamped shut, the doctor ran through a series of questions. They were similar to those Mrs Bagshaw and Tom had asked the night before and when she'd finished, she nodded. 'I agree with what your nurse guest and brother-in-law had to say. I don't think any harm has been done.'

Quinn's exhale of relief was audible, and Maggie Kinsella smiled. 'She's put you through it, hasn't she, Quinn?' Her eyes twinkled behind the glasses in Aisling's direction.

'We were both worried,' Quinn replied, squeezing Aisling's hand. 'And it feels like a lot has happened in the last twenty-four hours.'

He'd been so pale from lack of sleep and worry, Aisling thought as the colour seeped back into his cheeks. The tension between her shoulders dissipated despite Doctor Kinsella only having repeated what Mrs Bagshaw and Tom had told her the night before.

'Yes, quite. Finding out you're carrying twins is a lot to take on board for you both, but I'd say you were fortunate your, erm, tumble, last night wasn't more serious, especially having seen and, I have to say, admired your choice of footwear in the past, Aisling. It might be wise, however, to rethink your shoes for the interim.'

Aisling's face heated like a furnace. She felt like she was ten years old again, getting a telling off by one of the sisters at St Theresa's for having made what the nuns called the wrong choice. She'd chosen to stick chewing gum in Mary Mangan's ringlets because she'd been calling her Fanta and then giggling her head off with her friends. Mammy had told her to rise above it before trotting out the sticks and stones thing. However, seeing the chewing gum cut out of one of those fat brown ringlets had been far more satisfying.

'I'd suggest wearing flat shoes for the duration of your preg-nancy, and don't rush going up and down the stairs at the guesthouse, Aisling. Take your time.'

'I will.' Aisling wouldn't be doing anything to put the babies at risk. Still, she couldn't help frowning at the white trainers poking out of the bottom of the jeans she'd pulled on. She wondered if she'd get the same thrill of pleasure at seeing her Manola Blahnik's ever again.

That morning, as she'd pulled her socks on, she'd been worried whether her fat ankle would fit into her trainers, but there'd been the more pressing problem of locating the only pair of flat-soled shoes she owned in the first place. They'd not seen the light of day since she and Quinn had hired bikes and cycled around Phoenix Park. In the end, she'd got down on her hands and knees to search the bottom of her wardrobe, flinging out Valentino's, Dior's and her beloved Jimmy Choo's before seeing the ugly white shoes she was searching for stuffed at the back. She'd managed to get them on without bother and had hobbled forth with Quinn, feeling strange not being elevated by a stiletto, strange and short. Moira, who'd been on her knees tending to Kiera's nappy, had been quick off the mark, 'Good morning there, Grumpy.' Referencing Snow White's little friend. To which she'd replied, 'Feck off, Dopey.'

A laboriously slow journey down the stairs to reception had followed, where Aisling and Quinn were greeted by Bronagh, her mouth full of Special K. The spoon clattered down into the bowl as she spotted Aisling's limp and choice of footwear.

'What have you done to yourself?' she'd demanded, forgetting her breakfast as she stood up and marched, well, tried to—it wasn't easy in her pencil skirt, around the desk.

Aisling usually stood eye to eye with Bronagh, but she'd found herself looking up at her as she hesitated to respond. She didn't want to mention her reasons for coming downstairs the night before; not until she'd had the opportunity to check in with Freya about what had transpired with Sara Scott. Her head throbbed at the thought of the hotel inspector but seeing Bronagh's hands had moved to her hips, she replied, 'I called down to see how Freya was getting on last night and caught my heel in the carpet on the stairs there and took a little tumble.'

Bronagh pulled her to her bosom and then released her. 'Oh, Aisling,' Her forehead was creased with concern, and her black bob swung back and forth as she shook her head. She bit her vermillion-coloured bottom lip, anxiously awaiting the rest of the story.

'Don't say it, Bronagh. I've had all the lectures, which is why I'm wearing these.' She indicated the trainers.

'I was going to ask if you and the babbies are alright.'

'Sorry for jumping the gun,' Aisling replied, realising she'd sounded defensive. Bronagh had been over the moon upon hearing Aisling and Quinn's twin news yesterday. 'They are.' They had to be. 'I was lucky because Mrs Bagshaw, who happens to be a nurse, was on hand when it happened. She gave me the all-clear apart from a bruised ankle, so don't you be worrying now. Tom checked me over too.'

Quinn tugged at her arm. 'We've got to go, Bronagh. The doctor's squeezed us in so we can't be late.'

'It's just to be on the safe side,' Aisling reassured the receptionist as Quinn reached for the door. Then unable to help herself asked, 'Bronagh have you seen Sara Scott this morning?'

'I have as it happens. She checked out about forty minutes ago, and good riddance because we can all breathe again. I'd barely had time to hang my coat up, and she was standing at the front desk with her case at her feet.'

Oh dear, Aisling had thought, not getting the chance to respond as Quinn dragged her out of the door with him. She wished she'd at least been on hand to say goodbye to their undercover guest herself. She could have softened whatever the situation was that had upset Sara Scott before she left. It was too late now though. Que será, será she thought, whatever will be, will be.

Now, Doctor Kinsella got up from her chair and announced, 'I think we should have a look at that ankle, Aisling. You're walking on it, which is a good sign.' She moved around the desk while Aisling slid her foot out of her trainer, using her other foot to push the heel down. It was a habit that would have seen her get a telling off from Mammy. She pulled her sock off and tugged her jeans leg up so Doctor Kinsella could see it better. The bruising had come out overnight, and the GP took Aisling's foot in her hand, gently rotating it left and right. When she'd finished, she said, 'Well, Aisling, I think it's safe to say there's nothing broken or sprained and that it looks worse than it is. The best thing you can do for it is ice it every two to three hours for the next two days, keep it elevated as much as possible and rest it. A compression wrap will help ease the aching too.'

It was a relief to hear all this because when Aisling had clambered out of bed earlier, it had been tender to put weight on. She'd no wish to get about the place on crutches like Mammy had twice in recent history, especially given the stairs at O'Mara's. Worst-case scenario, she could go down them on her backside but getting back up them would have been interesting.

'I know how to wrap an ankle. I've seen my mam do my brother's enough times. Football,' Quinn supplied with a shrug.

'Good,' Doctor Kinsella said. 'And, once the bruising's gone, I think embarking on some gentle exercise could be good for you, Aisling. I know it's probably the last thing you feel like doing but walking or maybe swimming are helpful because exercise can help your body prepare for labour.'

Brilliant, Aisling thought. It was just like when she got her periods and had thought she'd a sure-fire excuse for the getting out of PE. No such luck.

Seeing Aisling pick up her sock, Maggie Kinsella straightened and said, 'Don't bother just yet, Aisling. I'd like you to hop up on the bed because I think it would put your minds at rest if we were to have a listen to the babies heartbeats.' She smiled at their enthusiasm as Aisling, forgetting her sore ankle, all but springboarded onto the bed, sweater up around her bra before the doctor had a chance to say another word.

Aisling's arms were by her sides and her hands clenched as she waited for Doctor Kinsella to fetch the equipment. She didn't realise her teeth were clenched until her jaw began to ache. At this rate, they'd be calling in at the dentist's too.

'Try and relax now, Aisling,' Doctor Kinsella instructed before apologising for the cold gel she was squeezing onto Aisling's abdomen.

The thing was, Aisling thought flinching at the sudden cold, when you were told to relax, your body automatically did the opposite. Still, she did her best by doing the heavy yoga breathing Rosi always recommended under times of stress. There was a sense of déjà vu because twenty-four hours earlier, she'd been in this same position breathing in the same sanitised smell all medical facilities seemed to possess. Quinn didn't want to get in the doctor's way but shuffled his seat a little closer anyway. He was doing the heavy yoga breathing too.

Doctor Kinsella ran what she'd explained was called a foetal doppler over Aisling's belly. After a few passes, as the heavy breathing got louder, all three smiled, hearing the unmistakable rhythm of a beating heart. Maggie Kinsella's head was tilted to one side as she continued moving the doppler across Aisling's stomach until she found what she was looking for. 'And there we are. The second heartbeat.'

Aisling burst into tears. Her jelly beans' heartbeats! It was the best sound she'd ever heard, and once Doctor Kinsella had wiped the gel off her stomach, passed her a tissue, and moved the equipment aside, she pulled her sweater down and sat up smiling through her tears. Quinn's eyes, too, were suspiciously bright.

As they left the surgery, Quinn paused for a moment. He took his wife by the shoulders. 'I love you, Aisling O'Mara-Moran.'

'I love you too, Quinn Moran.'

Their gazes softened, and Aisling wrapped her arms around Quinn's neck, not caring that his face was scratchy and unshaven as, standing on tippy-toes, she raised her head so their lips could meet. There was an urgency to the kiss, and the world around them faded until a shrill voice broke the spell, and they sprang apart as though they were teenagers caught by their mams and dads.

'This is a doctor's surgery car park. On your way, the pair of you.' An elderly woman waved them off with her walking stick turning to her younger companion to mutter, 'What's the world coming to, Fiona? I blame that new programme on television. The *Big Brother* one with the cameras watching when they're all at it. Disgusting, so it is. Your father would be turning in his grave.'

Quinn helped Aisling into the tank, and once he'd got behind the wheel, he looked at her. They burst out laughing.

Chapter Thirteen

♥

A isling was fed up with lounging around. There was only so much lying on the sofa a girl could do, and it wasn't nearly as much fun when snowballs weren't involved, but the thought of her go-to chocolate treat made her feel ill. It was irrelevant anyway because Moira would have snaffled what was left in the bag she'd stashed at the back of the kitchen cupboards even if she had been up for them.

Aisling was also desperate to know what mood Sara Scott had vacated the guesthouse in and what had got her upset the night before in the first place. It was playing on her mind, and her hand snaked out for the phone in easy reach on the coffee table, but she let it fall back down. She couldn't hear herself think with the current ruckus going on.

Poor Kiera didn't know what to do with herself, thanks to a new tooth making its presence known. She was sitting on the living room floor, bare-bottomed and grizzling. Aisling would have liked to have joined in with her grizzling. Not the bare bum bit.

Moira had given Aisling a blow-by-blow account of the last nappy Kiera had filled and how Mammy had been on at her about the importance of airing her bottom to avoid the nappy rash.

The little girl had been out of sorts all afternoon and had refused most of her dinner, choosing to slump in her high chair, rubbing her ears instead, and her cheeks were fiery. Moira looked frazzled and close to the edge as she picked up various toys tossing them in the playpen. 'I'll run her a bath in a minute. That usually calms her down, and then it will be time for a bottle and bed.'

Kiera raised her head and began to howl as though there was a moon on the ceiling.

'Shall I read her a story? While you run the bath,' Aisling offered, wishing she could make things better for her niece because it upset her seeing her like so.

'You can try.' Moira was too weary to be grateful, and she rifled through the stack of books in the corner of the pen. 'She likes this one.' *Brown Bear, Brown Bear, What do you See?* was frisbeed over to Aisling, who sat herself up in readiness. Moira abandoned the tidying up and picked Kiera up, carrying her over to the sofa. 'Auntie Aisling's going to read you the bear book while Mammy runs the bath.' Kiera wasn't impressed and was even less impressed when her mammy put her down on the sofa next to her aunt before fleeing towards the bathroom.

'Ma! Ma!' she sobbed out.

Aisling suspected it would take Moira ages to run the bath that evening. What would it be like for her when she had two little babbies teething like so? she wondered. Then, putting it out of her mind, she concentrated on the little babby sitting alongside her. 'This looks like a very good story, Kiera. I like bears,' Aisling said, opening the book.

Kiera slouched down, and Aisling caught her before she slid right off the sofa. She sat her niece on her lap where she could keep hold of her. 'So you're not in the mood for a story. Well, how about this then.' Aisling tweaked Kiera's chubby big toe and began reciting this little piggy nursery rhyme, but the howling only worsened. 'Mary had a little lamb then, or maybe Old MacDonald?' She desperately launched into a round of

Old McDonald had a farm and had just done the moo, moo here bit when the phone rang. 'What's the bet that's your nana?'

Kiera stopped sobbing hearing her beloved nana mentioned.

Please let it be nana, Aisling thought, answering.

It was.

'Mammy, Kiera's after cutting a tooth, and she's miserable. Poor Moira's at her wit's end. She's hiding in the bathroom, pretending she's running a bath. What should I do?'

'Put my little Princess Twinkle Toes on the phone, Aisling,' Maureen said, taking charge.

'Nana wants a word with you, Kiera.' Aisling dabbed the dribble from her chin with her bib, then held the phone near her ear, leaning in so she could listen.

'Hello, princess, it's your nana speaking. Poppy D and Nana will sing the "Islands in the Stream" song for you, and I'll play the tambourine, too. That always helps with those nasty toothy pegs, so it does, sweetheart!' Muffled voices sounded, and there was a shuffling as though the phone was being passed about.

'Poppa D is in da house!' Donal announced while Maureen shook the tambourine.

Kiera's sobbing had ebbed to the occasional judder and Aisling's eyes were wide as Donal and Mammy launched into Kenny and Dolly's famous duet. If she weren't seeing it with her own eyes, Aisling wouldn't have believed it. Mammy and Donal were the babby whisperers because Kiera's face was alight with delight. Her teeth and tears were forgotten as she was serenaded down the phone.

As the song drew to a close, Aisling pulled the phone away, and Kiera's face crumpled. 'Can you do the extended version, please?' she begged. 'I can hear the water running in the bathroom, but Moira's not ready yet.'

There was conferring down the line. Was Kiera as partial to a spot of Sheena and Kenny as she was the great man and Dolly?

'Do the islands one again. She loved that. Why fix something that's not broken,' Aisling said, putting in her two pennies' worth.

They were onto their third rendition when Moira finally appeared with a hooded baby towel slung over her arm looking quite zen as she glided over to collect her child. 'Who's on the phone?'

'Kenny and Dolly over there in the Howth. Honestly, Moira, they should cut a CD. They're ten times better than those Wiggles fellas.' Aisling pressed the phone to her ear. 'Thanks a million, you two. Kiera's going to have her bath now and Moira doesn't look like she's on the edge of a nervous breakdown anymore.' She said her goodbyes and hung up.

Moira hoisted Kiera on her hip. 'I rang Rosi on my mobile in the bathroom and I did the heavy yoga breathing while she talked me through, visualising I was sitting alongside a babbling brook in a tranquil field. The running bathwater helped. But it made me need to wee too.'

Aisling nodded and watched the pair of them disappear. She was alone. Quinn and Tom were both at the restaurant. For the first time since yesterday evening, she was alone. Surely it wouldn't do any harm to pop downstairs and find out what had transpired last night with Sara Scott? She knew sleep would be a waste of time if she didn't get to the bottom of it. Her eyes strayed to her foot which was wrapped tighter than an Egyptian mummy. It was only bruised, and she was fed up with staring at the same four walls, having done as she'd been told and rested it once she and Quinn had returned from the doctors.

Craning an ear, she heard splashing and giggling. How could that be the same child who'd been utterly miserable all day? Mammy and Donal were going to be in hot demand when the jelly beans came along alright. She wrapped her arms around her middle and tried to envisage them tucked away inside her, picturing them holding hands as they floated about. But then, on the television, an actress appeared who bore a faint resemblance to Freya, and that was that.

Moira and Kiera would still be a good twenty minutes or so in the bathroom. She hauled herself up and tested her weight on her foot. It felt much better, and if she went straight downstairs, spoke to Freya and came straight back up, no one need be any the wiser.

Aisling's mind was made up, and sneaking from the apartment, she carefully made her way down the stairs to reception. No one other than Freya was about and she didn't hear her approach as she inputted guest information into the computer.

'How're you, Freya?' she asked, pleased to see the young woman busily working through the pile of January bookings.

'Aisling!'

'Sorry, I didn't mean to make you jump.'

'I was concentrating on these.' She gestured to the paperwork and smiled at her employer. 'I never heard you coming down the stairs. It's good to see you, although Quinn said you're supposed to be resting your ankle?'

'I have been, and this is our little secret, alright?'

Freya nodded.

She'd a pretty shade of pink gloss on her lips tonight, Aisling noticed. It softened her because she was a pretty girl with hard edges. She was like Emer in that respect, but that was where the similarities ended from what Aisling had seen. 'I wanted to ask you what happened with Sara Scott last night.'

Freya's eyes shone earnestly. 'I am so sorry for asking you to come downstairs. I should have just spoken to you on the phone. You falling like that was my fault.'

Aisling held a hand up to stop her. 'It wasn't your fault at all. It was no one's fault.' Actually, it was hers, but she didn't need to get into that with Freya. 'It was an accident, and other than a few bruises, I'm none the worse for it.'

'Thank goodness.'

'Yes.' Aisling needed to get things moving along. 'So, Sara Scott?'

Freya shifted in her seat and looked uncomfortable. 'It was nothing. Honestly, I shouldn't have bothered you in the first place.'

'Freya,' Aisling said gently. 'I'm the manager of O'Mara's. If there's a problem with a guest, especially a guest I suspect of being a hotel inspector, then it's my job to fix it. Not yours. Do you understand?'

Freya dipped her head, and her lips moved from side to side in indecision before she finally spoke up. 'I didn't want to bother you with this because it's all been sorted out now. Bronagh said Ms Scott was happy when she left.'

Aisling waited, half expecting to hear Moira hollering over the balcony rail that if she didn't get back upstairs and rest her foot, she'd ring Quinn and tell on her.

'It was over a message for Ms Scott about dinner arrangements she was to make for her and her friend to dine at The Clarence. Bronagh forgot to pass it on, and of course, it was too late to get a table by the time Ms Scott heard from her friend again. I didn't think I should mention they'd never have been able to book a table at such short notice anyway. Not unless Naomi Campbell or the like was tagging along.'

'Quite right,' Aisling said, sighing. She'd hoped it wouldn't have had anything to do with Bronagh but a niggling worry as to why their efficient and long-serving receptionist was suddenly letting things slide had told her otherwise.

She felt sick. What was she going to do? It was so out of character, especially given Bronagh knew who Sara Scott was. She supposed she could talk to Mammy about it, but Mammy would be bound to want to speak to Bronagh to see what was going on. It would only upset her and quash her excitement about Leonard coming over for Christmas, which wouldn't be fair.

Aisling closed her eyes for a split second, feeling the beginnings of a headache, knowing she'd opt for the easy option and leave it be for the time being. 'I'm sorry it was left to you to sort out.'

Freya looked nervous. 'I made an executive decision. I hope you don't mind, but I organised a complimentary table for two at Quinn's and rang ahead to be sure they were made to feel extra special. When I explained the circumstances to Alasdair, he said he'd be sure to give them a good table and ensure they were well looked after. Given Ms Scott was in good humour when she checked out, I'd say she and her friend had an enjoyable evening.'

'That's what I call showing initiative, Freya. Well done.'

'You won't mention I told you about the forgotten message to Bronagh, will you? I'd hate for her to think I was telling tales.'

'You're not telling tales. You're telling the truth, and I won't say a word about it. I think Bronagh's in need of a good break. Sure she'll be back to her old self in the new year. You'll see. Now, I'd best get back up those stairs and let you get on with your bookings there.'

Freya smiled and wished her goodnight, turning her attention back to her forms with a satisfied smile at how things had played out.

Aisling's foot was aching by the time she crept back into the apartment to come face to face with Moira, who was standing hands on hips in the living room, looking uncannily like Mammy only instead of, And what time do you call this? she said, 'Where've you been then?'

'I ducked downstairs for a quick word with Freya.'

'You're supposed to be resting. Quinn told me I'm to make sure you do.'

'I am resting. See!' Aisling flopped down on the sofa.

'Not yet, you don't.' Moira marched over and took her sister's hand, pulling her back up. 'You can be Kenny, and I'll be Dolly.'

So it was the two sisters stood over Kiera's crib singing "Islands in the Stream" until, at last, the little girl's eyelids fluttered shut, and she fell asleep.

Chapter Fourteen

♥

Four Days Later

'There's ham in the fridge and baps in the freezer for your lunch, Donal, and you can heat yourself a bowl of the vegetable soup I made this morning. It's in the pot on the stove. Aisling and I will grab a bite in Howth. I'll ring you on my mobile when we're ready to be picked up,' Maureen said, draping her new burnt orange scarf around her neck.

'That's a pretty shade of orange, Mammy,' Aisling said, noticing the scarf matched her hat and coat. Mammy never did things by halves, she thought.

'Burnt orange, Aisling. Ciara with a C from my little boutique in Howth says it's all the rage this winter, and the colour looks very well on me.'

'Burnt orange then.' Aisling corrected herself. Moira was beginning to worry Ciara with a C, had been put in Mammy's Will. She buys her cakes and everything, she'd said, sobering between sniggering over Aisling's excursion into Howth for special shoes. We need to keep an eye on her, or she'll be doing our children out of their rightful inheritance. You watch, Moira had continued. The next time Moira sniggered, Aisling told her that at least she wouldn't have to pay for whatever shoes were bought today. That had wiped the smile off Moira's face, and depositing her daughter on her aunt's knee, she'd rung her mammy quick smart to see if she would spring for the special coat she'd seen in the window of Brown Thomas the other day. Mammy told her there was nothing wrong with the coat she had.

Donal looked up from where he was sitting at the table with the Saturday morning paper spread out in front of him and, peering over the top of his reading glasses which had slipped halfway down his nose, said, 'I'll be ready when you're ready, Mo. And soup and a bap will set me up nicely for band practice this afternoon.' With the house to himself for the morning, he planned on putting his favourite country music CD compilation on and pushing the boat out with a second brew of the Irish Crème plunger coffee that was his and Maureen's favourite Saturday morning caffeine fix. She liked them to limit their consumption to just one pot, but what she didn't know wouldn't hurt her. A thought occurred to him. 'Did you put garlic in the soup?' The last time she made soup, she'd used nearly a whole bulb to ward off winter's coughs and colds. He'd not been popular with his bandmates.

'Just a smidgen, Donal.' Maureen demonstrated a smidgen by rubbing her index finger and thumb together.

He smiled. 'Grand, that colour's lovely on you, so it is.' Donal locked eyes with his live-in lady friend, who began to do the woolly burnt orange scarf version of the dance of the seven veils in response.

Aisling coughed lest they forget she was in the room. It wasn't an enjoyable experience bearing witness to her mammy being flirtatious with a scarf. But, as it was, she was here under duress. She'd felt rough since she got up, and despite ever-present nausea, she'd prefer to be jogging the Grand Canal route with Quinn and Tom than going special shoe shopping in Howth with Mammy. Given Aisling didn't jog, not ever, this said a lot. After the other night, however, she was in no position to argue about footwear. So when Mammy had telephoned her to lock in a Saturday morning shopping expedition, she'd reluctantly agreed. On the bright side, it would be an excellent opportunity to broach her worries about Bronagh away from the guesthouse.

Maureen stopped flicking her scarf at Donal and turned to Aisling, who was slipping into her coat. 'Have you a vest on under that sweater?'

'Yes, Mammy and I've tucked it into my knickers.'

'I'm surprised you can tuck anything in, given the knickers you and your sisters wear. It can't be comfortable getting around like one of those sumo wrestlers with the cloth up the bottom like so. Next time I'm in Marks and Spencers, I'll pick you up some proper knickers. It's not right wearing the wispy string things when you're with babbies.'

Donal rustled the papers loudly.

Aisling was trying to see over her shoulder because she didn't like the sumo wrestler bottom reference but giving up, she belted her jacket. Then glancing down sighed. She looked like Minnie Mouse with her trainers peeping out from under the hem of her jeans. It was a look Moira had perfected back in her Mason Price days when she'd walk to the law firm, changing shoes once she'd slid behind the reception desk. It wasn't a look Aisling had ever embraced before today, and Minnie Mouse was preferable to Goofy, which was what she had a feeling she'd be looking like before the morning was over.

Once Pooh was on his lead and Maureen had made sure her mobile phone was in her handbag, they headed for the front door. Aisling called out goodbye to Donal, bracing herself for the day waiting for them outside the toasty house. It was her fault, she thought. She'd made the mistake of relaying Doctor Kinsella's comments about gentle exercise being good preparation for labour. So now they were rugging up to brave the elements and stroll into Howth. So far as Maureen O'Mara was concerned, Doctor Maggie Kinsella's word was gospel.

It wasn't too bad for December, Aisling thought, standing on the gravel and looking up at a sky that, while grey, wasn't ominous. A sharp wind was blowing, but the blast of fresh air straight off the Atlantic relieved the wooziness. Not that she had any intention of admitting this to her mammy, she thought, hurrying to catch up with her and Pooh, who were already halfway down the drive.

The trio had settled into a comfortable pace as they made their way down the hill towards the village shops. Aisling was marvelling over how many times Pooh had cocked a leg in the short time since they'd left the house. Did he store it up especially for walks because he'd peed against everything from shrubs, letter boxes and lamp posts? He'd even attempted a short wee against a fellow dog walker's trouser leg, but Mammy had given him short shrift. Pooh, not the dog walker. 'Get your arms moving, Aisling,' she was trilling now like a bossy Butlins Red Coat and was so busy demonstrating the arms swinging she nearly smacked a fellow pedestrian, attempting to overtake them on the left, in the face. Aisling gave her arms a little swing once the woman had hurried on and was a safe distance ahead of them.

'Put more into it!'

Aisling frowned. She felt like an eejit but did as Mammy had said anyway.

'That's it. Now get your hips moving too.'

And so it was mother and daughter cleared a path along the bustling pavement of Howth's main street as they strode along with a poodle in tow, looking as though they were competing in the racewalking at the Commonwealth games.

Maureen, spying her favourite café across the road, slowed her pace. 'I'll pick up a little something sweet for Ciara, I think. Her mammy doesn't feed her properly.' She made a disapproving clucking sound. 'You know, you girls don't know how lucky you are to have a Mammy that always made sure you'd eaten everything on your plate when you were children.'

Aisling hadn't felt lucky when she'd been staring at the clump of boiled yellow broccoli. On the contrary, she'd felt very unlucky, as Mammy had informed her children were starving in Africa. Children who'd give their eye teeth for a piece of broccoli and that she'd not be leaving the table until she'd got it down her. However, she didn't think it was wise to voice this as they waited for a break in the traffic. It was crawling past in a continual flow. 'In Vietnam, they just walk out into the road,' Maureen stated, one leg outstretched. 'All the little motorbikes veer around yer.'

Aisling yanked her back. 'You're in Howth, Mammy, not Hanoi. You'll get mowed down if you're not careful. The crossing's just up there.' So, with her mammy wittering on about pig-ignorant drivers and daughter who was with babbies, they reached the crossing and made it safely across the road to the café.

'I won't be long. Do you want to come in or wait out here with Pooh?'

'I'll wait out here, Mammy,' Aisling replied, taking the lead from her.

Maureen studied her daughter's face, 'Do you know you've the colour back in your cheeks and a sparkle in your eye, so you do. That walk did you a world of good.'

Aisling felt good, and sniffing the salt air made her think of hot chips. She watched her mammy disappear inside the café and then let Pooh pull her over to the bowl of water the owners of the café always left out for dogs. Chips, chips, chips, she chanted to herself, amazed that the thought of something other than toast and ginger biscuits wasn't making her feel sick for the first time in three months. She hoped Mammy bought her a cake too because she had a feeling she'd enjoy it. A cake with fresh cream in it would hit the spot. In the meantime, she'd a phone call to be making.

Pooh was drinking lustily as though he'd traversed the Sahara and emerged at an oasis. Aisling knew from watching his leg cocking on the walk down the hill he wasn't dehydrated, still and all she wouldn't mind a drink herself and wished she'd had a fancy water bottle like Quinn's with her. Ah well, a walk down a hill was hardly on the same par as jogging the ten-mile circuit he and Tom had planned today. Wondering how they were getting on, she fetched her mobile phone from her jacket pocket, and a moment later, Moira's breathless voice answered hello.

'Moira, it's me, Aisling.'

'For feck's sake, Ash, you're spending too much time with Mammy. I know it's you. Your name comes up on the screen. What do you want?'

'That's a charming way to talk to your pregnant sister. What have you been up to all out of puff, like?'

'Andrea invited myself and Kiera over to see her new flat.'

'That's nice. You two haven't caught up for a while.' Moira and Andrea had been thick as thieves when they both worked at Mason Price. Their lives had gone down different paths, but Aisling was glad they kept in touch. She'd already found out that maintaining long-term friendships could be tricky when your lives veered off in different directions. The key was finding a middle ground because you might be a parent or about to become one, but that didn't mean you stopped being a person in your own right. Moira was whispering, and she had to strain to hear what she was saying over the noise of the passing cars.

'It's a nightmare, Ash. You've no idea, but you will soon enough when you've Moira and Tom Junior to be running around after. Your friends that don't have children haven't a clue. I tell you absolutely everything of value Andrea owns is at the perfect height for Kiera to snatch and grab.'

'Moira! My babbies will not be named after you and Tom. Get it out of yer head.'

'Junior, don't forget the junior. And why are you ringing?' Moira cut to the chase.

'I'm outside the café. You know the one with the nautical theme that almost makes you feel seasick when you sit at the tables.'

'The one with the piratey man behind the counter?'

'How many cafés with a nautical theme do you think there are in Howth, Moira?'

'I was just checking. And why are you outside the café, not inside it?'

'Because Mammy's after calling in to pick up something sweet for Ciara with a C.'

'No!'

'Yes!'

'If it's a cream slice, we've got trouble.'

'She's coming.' Aisling disconnected the call.

'Who were you talking to?' Maureen asked, a paper bag held carefully in her hand.

'Moira. She wanted to know if we'd bought the shoes yet.'

Maureen didn't pick up on the fib. 'Sure, we've plenty of time for the shoes. We'll call in on Ciara with the slice first.'

Aisling and Pooh trailed after Maureen.

'Mammy?'

'Yes, Aisling?'

'What sorta slice is it?'

'Cream.'

'And did you buy two?'

'No. Sure, what would be the point in that. I'm watching my weight, and you've no appetite on you.'

Feck, Aisling thought. They had trouble alright.

Chapter Fifteen

♥

'Now, this is new in. Burnt orange would work well with your colouring Aisling and the cut offers plenty of room for expansion in the upcoming months.' Ciara plucked the dress off the one size fits all rack and held it out for Maureen and Aisling to see. She'd got over her annoyance at being interrupted as she browsed the latest *Marie Claire* magazine she'd picked up on her lunch break when Maureen presented her with a cream slice.

'Lovely,' Maureen murmured.

It reminded Aisling of a sari. Not that there was anything wrong with a sari. They were beautiful, but Aisling wasn't a sari sort of a girl.

Maureen's face lit up like a Christmas tree as she turned to Aisling and said, 'We could twin in the burnt orange.'

Jaysus wept! Aisling thought, looking like she'd trodden in something Pooh had deposited in the garden. Twinning with Mammy? She'd never hear the end of it from Moira and Rosi.

'And, because it drapes over one shoulder like so, you can wear a polo neck under it now for warmth, and when you get ginormous over the summer, you can wear it on its own. So if you look at it that way, you're getting a two-for-one dress,' Ciara chirped.

'Now that's what I call bang for your buck.' Maureen nodded approvingly. 'Ciara here knows what she's talking about, Aisling.' She reached out to stroke the voluminous fabric.

Bang for your buck? Where had Mammy picked up that particular Americanism? Aisling wondered, cringing inwardly. Still, she supposed punch for your punt didn't have the same ring. She stared aghast at the burnt orange-coloured sari dress Ciara was holding up. It would be beautiful worn for the right occasion but strutting about a Dublin guesthouse in daylight, wasn't it. Her stomach sank with the realisation that no matter how much she protested that she just wasn't a burnt orange, twinning sorta gal, she'd be leaving the shop with the dress in a bag. Mammy had that determined glint in her eyes, and dragging her gaze from the sari dress to Ciara, she saw she did too.

'Why don't you try it on?' Maureen enthused.

Aisling scrambled for a plausible excuse. 'Ah no, Mammy. Sure, Quinn and I have twins on the way. That's enough twinning for the time being, and two babbies means two of everything, so I don't need to be splashing the cash on new dresses.' She'd glimpsed the price tag and it was eye-watering.

'Aisling O'Mara, aren't we after having a mammy-daughter day out?'

'O'Mara-Moran, Mammy.'

'It's my treat, so it is.' Maureen ignored her.

'But, Mammy, if you buy this for me, Moira will be at you for the coat she's got her eye on, and Rosi won't want to miss out either.'

'Are they giving their mammy twins? No, they are not, and you said it yourself. You're having two babbies which means you'll be enormous in a few months. I don't know what you think you'll be getting about in but take it from someone who's been there and done that four times. You won't want to feel restricted in your clothes.'

'You never had twins, Mammy.'

'No, that's true, but given the size of you girls' pumpkin heads, I might as well have.' Maureen grimaced at the memories, and Ciara gave a sympathetic tut.

'Sure, I've my Mo-pants, Mammy. They've plenty of stretch in them, so they do, and you know yourself they can be dressed up or down.'

'They won't stretch to a beach ball being stuck down them,' Maureen muttered darkly. 'C'mon now. No arguing. I think you'd get plenty of wear out of this. And it will be lovely getting out and about in matching colours. People will think we're mammy and daughter.'

'We are mammy and daughter,' Aisling said, watching as her mammy took the dress from Ciara and made a beeline for the changing room, where she hung it up.

'And burnt orange is this season's colour, isn't it, Ciara? Just because you're with babbies doesn't mean you have to look frumpy. It's not like it was in my day when we just cut a hole out of our skirts to make room.'

Aisling was not sold. Ciara had told Mammy that burnt orange suited her too, and she and Aisling were opposites in the colouring department. Mammy would joke Aisling was the milkman's when she was young, which wasn't very funny given he had the reddish hair.

Aisling had inherited Nanna Dee's, on her dad's side, colouring with her strawberry-blonde hair, freckles, green eyes and fair skin, while Mammy turned a gorgeous mahogany in summer and had eyes as dark as her hair. So, while the dress might be one size fits all, she didn't believe orange was a one colour suits all, even if it was burnt. But Ciara was nodding enthusiastically.

'It's all about BO this winter, as we in the trade call it. Look, it says so in here!' Ciara jabbed at her *Marie Claire* magazine, still open on the counter.

'It says so in the fashion magazine, Aisling. So there you go.' Maureen told her daughter.

'Might I say that hat, coat and scarf look well on you, Maureen?'

'Well, now I think we know who to thank for that, don't we?' Maureen flicked her scarf back over her shoulder, and the two women giggled.

Jaysus wept. Anyone would think Ciara was her mammy's fifth born child the way the pair of them were carrying on, Aisling thought, frowning. Moira was right, and it was worse for her because her position as the baby in the family was at risk of being usurped. Ciara was a cuckoo in the nest, and she wished she'd pushed that cream slice she'd gobbled down into her cheek-boney face. It was annoying enough that she could stuff cakes down and still look like Kate Moss, but her proprietorial air with Mammy was even more annoying.

The thing was, Maureen O'Mara didn't listen to anyone. Certainly not her daughters, but for whatever reason, she'd decided Ciara with a 'C' was her guru regarding fashion. Aisling blamed the wrap dress, Mammy had bought from her. That's when it started. She closed her eyes for a second, picturing herself with a cream pie like in the old *Laurel and Hardy* silent films, then opened her eyes and sighed, knowing she'd not be throwing any pies at Ciara because she'd be too busy eating them. She was ravenous. The appetite that had deserted her these last months was back with a vengeance. As such, she'd have to be satisfied with the younger woman sporting a cream moustache which Mammy hadn't pointed out because she'd forgotten her glasses. Something which also meant she'd yet to see the price tag of the sari dress she was insisting Aisling try on.

Maureen and Ciara had stopped giggling and were now gazing at Aisling expectantly.

There was nothing else for it. She was fighting a losing battle. Aisling knew the sooner they got out of this place, the sooner they'd go and get her shoes, and then, at last, she'd be able to have lunch. Accordingly, she marched into the fitting room and wrenched the curtain closed. 'Don't you dare open it, Mammy. I'll come out when I'm good and ready.' The memory of purchasing her first bra at thirteen years of age was still raw. There she'd been in the department store's fitting room about to try on one of the bras Mammy had picked out for her, guessing at her size, when the curtain had been pulled open, revealing her bare budding breasts to the entire underwear section. A matronly figured woman whose own bosoms you could rest a cup of tea on, so good was her support, was standing next to her mammy, measuring tape in hand. It had been mortifying.

Now, she hung her jacket on the hook before slipping out of her jeans and sweater. The sight of her vest tucked into her knickers made her grimace. A shadow appeared under the curtain. 'Don't even think about it, Mammy,' Aisling hissed.

'It's me, Ciara. I have a polo neck for you to wear underneath the dress.'

'Let me guess. In BO.' BO was precisely what she thought of this season's hottest shade.

'I've managed to match it exactly.'

'Great.' Aisling's teeth were gritted as she snaked her hand around the side of the curtain to fetch the knit.

'Sure, I don't know what's got you behaving all coy-like,' Maureen announced too close to the fitting room for Aisling's liking. 'We're all girls together, and you've no problem strutting about the pool in the skimpy swimsuit. You want to have seen her when we were in Los Angeles, Ciara. She'd no shame.'

'Just back away from the fitting room. Both of you, or I won't come out.' Aisling waited until the shadows disappeared to wriggle into the polo neck first before dropping the dress down over her head. 'Christ on a bike,' she breathed, taking stock of the burnt orange apparition in the mirror. Mary Mangan's childhood taunt came back to her. 'You look like a one-litre-sized bottle of Fanta.' It was hard to imagine she'd ever be big enough to fill the dress out that from the bust down was so roomy two women could get about in it happily. But then she thought back to how enormous Moira had become in her pregnancy's latter stages and doubled it. No, she still couldn't imagine it. She angled for a side-on in the mirror to see if it was any better, hearing Mammy and Ciara's voices drifting under the curtain.

'How's that nice young man of yours, Paul?'

'Pete. And he wasn't nice. He had terrible dandruff. We broke up.'

'Oh, I'm sorry to hear that, but as my girls know, Ciara, you've got to kiss a few frogs before you find your prince. Isn't that right, Aisling?'

'Whatever you say, Mammy.' She pulled a face. Side-on was even worse.

'Are you decent?'

For feck's sake, she nearly pulled the curtain from its track as she whipped it open and stepped out of the fitting room to where Mammy and Ciara were waiting.

'Oh, you're a picture.' Maureen clapped her hands delightedly. 'I can always rely on you to find just the thing, Ciara.'

Ciara preened. 'I could tell from Aisling's pear shape that the dress would suit her, Maureen.'

I'd rather be a pear than a fecking... she couldn't think of any straight up and down skinny fruit, and Mammy was asking her to give them a twirl. She did so with a scowl firmly in place.

'Not so heavy on the feet, Aisling. She was the same when she did the ballet lessons, stomping about the place like she should be doing the fee-fi-fo-fum instead of the sugar plum fairy.' Maureen moved to stand next to Aisling.

'You two look like sisters.' Ciara smiled, knowing she would make the sale and keep her boss, Shirley, happy. She was also eager to get this show back on the road so she could return to her magazine.

'Twins,' Maureen exclaimed happily, already delving into her bag for her purse. 'Why don't you stay in your new outfit, Aisling. It's much smarter than what you had on.'

Aisling opened her mouth to protest, but Ciara had produced a pair of scissors seemingly from thin air and was stalking towards her.

Maureen was twittering on about the special shoes they were off to buy next which would be the finishing touch to Aisling's Saturday morning makeover, while Aisling retrieved her clothes from the fitting room. She slipped her jacket on over the top of her new outfit wishing she'd worn a coat which would have covered it. Ciara was already behind the till waiting for Maureen to zip-zap her card in the machine.

The explosive coughing from Maureen as Ciara smiled sweetly and told her the total price for the BO sari dress and polo neck suggested she no longer felt as though she were getting bang for her buck. Aisling smirked, knowing her honorary daughter position had been revoked. Leaving the shop assistant still with her cream moustache, they exited the boutique.

She was conspicuous in her billowing BO dress amongst the Saturday morning shoppers and daytrippers. It was a dress that would be more at home wafting around the grounds of Enya's castle over there in Killiney. Thinking of Killiney made her think of one of the singer's neighbours, Bono, and that wouldn't do at all. Moira had threatened her poor babbies with the 'Beautiful Day' song if she didn't let her borrow her boots the other day. She'd even begun to sing the first few lines at the top of her lungs. Aisling had no choice but to give in. She couldn't be having little Bono fan babbies, and shuddering at the memory, she pulled her jacket around her. That wind was freezing.

Pooh, they saw, was being subjected to the attentions of a frisky corgi. Maureen explained to the corgi owner, who could have auditioned for the role of Sherlock Holmes had he added a pipe to his outfit, that the little dog was barking up the wrong tree because Pooh had been seen to, and it would take more than a wiggle and a waggle to get him going.

Sherlock and his short-legged pooch got on their way, leaving Maureen to untie Pooh.

'Where is this shoe shop exactly, Mammy?' Aisling couldn't recall ever having seen a cobbler's shop in Howth.

Maureen touched the side of her nose and said, 'Cobbler's, Aisling, and it's a local secret. Although the way word's spreading about Rosemary's special boots and how she's like a mountain goat these days getting about the Howth hills, I don't think it will stay that way.'

She set off down the street.

Aisling followed, pausing as she saw Maeve Binchy's *Scarlet Feather* on display in the bookshop window. She loved the Queen of Irish fiction's books and was about to call after her mammy to wait while she nipped in to buy it only to realise she'd disappeared. How odd. And, taking a few steps in the direction they'd been headed, thought a woman and her poodle couldn't just vanish off a bustling main street on a Saturday morning, surely? But vanish, it would seem, they had.

Chapter Sixteen

♥

Aisling pressed her lips together, annoyed. She'd only had her back turned for a few seconds, and Mammy had disappeared. A harried woman wrapped in a camel-coloured coat who looked around her age was walking towards her. She'd a girl of about eight, zipped into an anorak, in tow who was wearing a face that said her mammy had told her no to ice cream. I'll ask them if they've seen a little woman in burnt orange with a poodle, Aisling decided, stepping into their path, but before opening her mouth, the woman pulled her daughter into her side. She glared at Aisling and said, 'We're Catholic. So we won't be needing the Hare Krishna books today, thank you!' They hurried on their way, and an indignant Aisling carried on up the street.

Her hair whipped around her face, and she tucked it behind her ears, but it was a lost cause, as it would seem was her hunt for Mammy and Pooh. However, as a rogue wind gusted down the street sending Aisling's dress flying up around her ears, she forgot all about them. It was like a scene from Marilyn Monroe's film, *The Seven Year Itch*, only instead of a white halter neck dress, Aisling was wearing a burnt orange sari dress, and she wasn't standing over a New York subway grille but instead on the Howth pavement.

She was busy trying to bat her dress down when two lads exiting a pub a few doors down where they'd partaken of a hair of the dog pint emerged and began elbowing one another. The one who was channelling Liam Gallagher and needed to wash his hair put his fingers in his mouth and let rip with a piercing wolf whistle. Aisling would have told them to feck off away with themselves, but she couldn't see them with the sari dress up around her ears. They'd mooched on their way by the time she'd wrested it under control to see she was not alone.

'You pay them no mind, dear,' the woman on the motorised scooter said kindly. 'I'm forever after telling my girls to tuck their vests into their knickers like so. You're a young lady who's got her head screwed on, so you are.' She gave Aisling a cheery smile, revved her engine and pootled on.

By now, Aisling's face was clashing with her dress, and she was about to take refuge inside the nearest shop when she saw it. A mirage-like laneway she'd never noticed before nestling between a vibrantly painted green building on its left and a red building on the right—an escape route! She swerved down it, glad of her trainers on the cobbles and came face to face with Mammy, who was straightening from having tethered Pooh. Aisling flew towards her full of blustering righteousness, 'I didn't know where you'd got to, Mammy! I've just been mistaken for a Hare Krishna, and now all of Howth knows I'm after tucking my vest into my knickers.' She paused to look about her. 'And, where did this lane come from. I've walked along the main street loads of times and never noticed it.'

'It's always been here, Aisling, and calm down because the wind will change and your face will stay like that.'

'Don't talk to me about the wind, Mammy. This dress is like a fecking sail when the wind catches it.'

Maureen looked hard at her daughter. 'If I didn't know better, I'd say you'd been at the wacky backy because Roisin talked a load of rubbish too when I caught her smoking the funny cigarette that time.'

Speaking of Roisin, Aisling heard her sister's voice in her head telling her to inhale for a count of three and exhale for a count of four. Or was it five? She couldn't remember, but either way, she'd regrouped by the fifth inhale.

Put what just happened behind you, Aisling, she told herself, still using Rosi's annoying yoga voice. Then, she checked out the gold-lettered sign for Carrick's the Cobbler's thinking the olde worlde shop reminded her of the picture book she had at home, *The Elves and the Shoemaker*. So, what footwear horrors lay behind the door she was about to follow her mammy through? And how much worse could this day get anyway? She'd soon find out, she thought, stepping inside the cobbler's shop.

To her surprise, the interior was spacious. It was also deserted and smelled of old leather, putting Aisling in mind of fuddy-duddy aftershaves that should have pipe tobacco mingling with them. The shelves were well stocked, and her gaze honed in on the selection of women's shoes and boots which weren't exactly Jimmy Choo's but weren't terrible either. A ray of hope shone on her tattered nerves. Perhaps a pair of special shoes wouldn't be so bad after all.

Maureen cocked an ear and frowned. 'Something's amiss. It's too quiet.' There was none of the usual banging and hammering coming from the workroom out the back, nor could she hear a radio. Although, as she strained now, she thought she'd heard whispering. She moved towards the counter where there was no sign of life and picked up the bell next to the til, giving it a vigorous shake. 'Yoo-hoo, Cathal!'

There was no reply other than Aisling's muttered, 'Jaysus, Mammy,' as she winced at the sudden bellow.

The silence was deafening.

Maureen leant across the counter and, turning back to face Aisling, brandished a lethal-looking weapon at her. 'I'll count to ten and if Cathal doesn't come out, I'm going in.'

'You could hurt someone with that, Mammy. Put it down. He might be in the jacks or something. You said yourself, Cathal and Rosemary were otherwise engaged out the back when you last called in.'

'I happen to know Rosemary's at the indoor bowls and that's the idea, Aisling. Why do you think I'm doing the countdown? It will give him plenty of time if he's after paying a visit. Sure, I'm only after watching an episode of *A Touch of Frost* where something similar happened.' Maureen bared her teeth fiercely in preparation.

'You don't need a weapon. That face would do the trick. And what do you mean where something similar happened?'

'There was a robbery. And it's not a laughing matter. You read about this sorta thing in the papers all the time.' She paused, wondering if the act of bravery she was about to commit would see her face splashed across the papers and wished she'd made an appointment to get her hair done earlier in the week. 'Ten, nine, eight, seven, six, five, four, three, two, one. I'm coming in!' She slowly advanced towards the workroom.

The way the day was unfolding, Aisling thought, she'd not be surprised if they had disturbed a robbery in progress. Well, she wouldn't be risking her babies. Mammy could take them on herself with whatever that sharp, pointy yoke was she had in her hand. She didn't doubt it would be the robbers who'd come out worst off if it came to it.

The door to the workroom flew open just as Mammy's arm stretched out to nudge it, making them jump.

'Jesus, Mary and Joseph, Maureen! Why are you pointing an awl at me?' A rumpled Cathal Carrick demanded. 'There's no need for that sorta carry-on Maureen. I'm sure you'll be more than happy with your boots.'

Maureen's arm dropped to her side. 'I thought you were being robbed out the back there. It was so quiet, but then I heard whispering and pictured all manner of things. None of them was good. I was set to burst in on the burglars when you appeared. Holy God above tonight, my heart's going like the clappers.'

Aisling decided she'd have a word with Donal about lowering Mammy's television crime drama consumption.

'You were coming to my rescue?' Cathal asked.

Maureen nodded. 'I was.'

Aisling was rapidly losing interest in the exchange now it was clear there was no robbery, and she picked up a pair of loafers, giving them a desultory once-over.

'Well, that's very kind of you, Maureen. Now, if you could pass me the awl you've got in your hand there, I'll fetch your new boots for you.'

Once disarmed, Maureen went and flopped down on the wooden chair where customers could sit when trying shoes. The adrenalin was no longer surging, and she was feeling a tad weak but perked up moments later when Cathal presented her with her new hiking boots. She was back to her old self when he said it would be rude of him not to offer her a twenty per cent discount under the circumstances.

'That's very good of you, so it is, Cathal.' Maureen slipped her boots off, eager to try the special ones on.

Aisling cleared her throat.

'Oh, and this is my middle daughter, Aisling.'

Aisling smiled at the cobbler, wondering how he could make all these different styles of shoes yet couldn't manage to do his shirt up properly. The buttons were all skew-whiff.

'They fit like a glove, Cathal,' Maureen said once she had the new boots on. 'We're having a mammy-daughter day, and given Aisling's expecting twins in the summer, we're after some special shoes for her today, please.' She did her laces up, simultaneously telling Cathal the story of the trip down the stairs because of the ridiculously high heels Aisling insisted on wearing.

When the cobbler could finally get a word in, he looked past Maureen to Aisling, whose eyes had glazed over. 'We met at the housewarming party, I do believe?'

His smile only made him look more elfin, Aisling thought, blinking. 'We did. It's nice to see you again, Mr Chinky.' She realised what she'd said upon seeing Mammy and the cobbler staring at her. 'Sorry! I meant Mr Carrick.'

'She's with the babbies,' Maureen said, tapping the side of her head with her index finger.

'I thought that was you I could hear, Maureen,' a familiar voice called from the workroom. A split second later, the plunk of Rosemary Farrell's hiking pole sounded before the woman appeared, looking as though she'd been dragged through a hedge.

'You told me you were at the indoor bowls this morning.' Maureen took stock of Cathal's shirt and the dishevelled state of Rosemary's usually sleek helmet hair. Her eyes narrowed, and her lips puckered prudishly. There was nothing wrong with Rosemary's hips today then, she thought. Her friend's carry-on these days made Bold Brenda look like the Virgin Mary.

'I planned on going, but I was waylaid.'

'I'll say.'

As for Aisling, it was too much, what with having been subjected to her mammy doing the dance of the seven veils with her burnt orange scarf for Donal earlier, the being mistaken for a Hare Krishna, and knicker-tucked-into-vest flashing episode, and now Rosemary Farrell looking like she should be lying back and lighting a cigarette. The ground felt as if it were wobbling and, fanning herself, she tried to loosen the polo neck, which had grown tight around her neck.

Cathal spotting her pale face, was quick to react, dashing over to tip Maureen from her chair so Aisling could sit down. Maureen took it as a cue to test the boots, and she set off at a clip around the shop.

'Thanks a million.' Aisling sank onto the seat.

'How're you, Aisling?' Rosemary asked, oblivious to her little episode. 'Your mammy's after telling me your news. Congratulations to you and Quinn.You'll have your hands full in a few months, so you will. You've saved me the price of a stamp calling in today because I've got a card in my purse for you both.' Rosemary disappeared out the back once more before Aisling could thank her while Maureen continued her circuits of the shop.

'Mammy, would you stop. You're making me dizzy.'

Maureen slowed and then came to a reluctant standstill. 'They're grand, so they are.' She inspected her new footwear, knowing she'd give Rosemary a run for her money across the rolling Howth hillside in them.

Rosemary returned with an envelope which she thrust at Aisling, 'No need to open it now.'

Aisling duly put it in her bag as Rosemary added, 'And I've already started knitting for the babbies. Yellow and green booties.' Then sizing the two women up, she announced, 'Did you know you're wearing matching colours?'

'It's called burnt orange, Rosemary or BO to those in the biz, and it's this season's colour trend,' Maureen said in a know-it-all sort of way that had Rosemary bristling.

Cathal said, 'Rosemary, why don't you tell Maureen all about the aqua-jogging you're thinking about trying at the Aquatic Centre while I see to Aisling?'

'What's aqua-jogging?' Maureen took the bait, bending down to take off the hiking boots. She'd not be traversing the countryside today.

Rosemary, pleased to tell Maureen something she didn't already know, took a deep breath to explain while Cathal asked Aisling to take off her trainers so he could measure her foot. He donned a pair of glasses and pulled a tape measure from his pocket.

Aisling caught snippets from Rosemary about flotation belts and jogging the length of the pool while Cathal measured both the length and width of her sock-clad feet. It sounded horrific.

'I take it you like height in your footwear, Aisling?' he asked, checking his measurements.

'I do,' Aisling replied wistfully. 'But I'll have to wear those old yokes for the next six months.' She gestured to her discarded trainers.

'Ah, now. I think we can do a little better than trainers.'

'You do?'

'I do. Just give me a minute or two.' He got up, taking himself out to his workroom.

Aisling tuned in to Rosemary and her mammy's conversation once more, then wished she hadn't.

'Aqua-jogging sounds just the ticket for Aisling, Rosemary. The doctor's after saying gentle exercise like swimming or walking's good for her and the babbies.'

'Swimming, Mammy, not running in the water,' Aisling quickly said.

''Tis very good for the pregnant women, I hear,' Rosemary replied to Maureen as though Aisling hadn't spoken.

'Moira could join us too and your Fenella. A girls' outing to the swimming pool. It'll be great craic.'

'Oh, Fenella's far too busy with the rhythmic gymnastics for aqua-jogging,' Rosemary replied loftily.

Aisling had no chance to repeat that she would not be joining them on their mammy-daughter aqua-jogging jaunt either because Cathal returned at that moment. He was holding out a pair of shoes that saw her mouth drop open. They weren't what she'd expected, and she held first her left foot and then her right foot aloft as though awaiting a glass slipper.

The cobbler eased them onto her feet, and she wiggled her toes to show him she'd plenty of room. The black leather slip-ons were light as air and soft as butter, and Aisling stayed seated, admiring the sparkling, silver diamante studs decorating the toes as they caught the light. These shoes were not the clodhoppers she'd envisaged, but the biggest surprise was yet to come.

Aisling stood up instantly, feeling as though she'd grown several inches. How could that be, though, because the slightly wedged heels were hardly high?

'It's the hidden support,' Cathal informed her.

He was a cobbler and magician, Aisling decided before setting off to do circuits of the shop.

Chapter Seventeen

♥

Two weeks later

Quinn placed the bowl in front of Aisling, and she dipped her spoon into the creamy porridge. Mmm, she mumbled, savouring the first mouthful of the breakfast. It was the perfect blend of salty and sweetness, but best of all, it was made with love.

Her eyes drifted to where Quinn was filling his water bottle at the kitchen sink, and then she began scooping her oats up as though she'd just completed a three-month dietary detox. She'd felt this way every day since the morning, afternoon, or whatever it was called sickness had stopped.

'I've got three months of eating to catch up on, Moira,' she'd garbled through a mouthful of honey toast when Moira pass-remarked that she was getting as bad as Kiera for stuffing things in her mouth. 'I'm eating for three, you know,' she'd added for good measure, having decided this would be her catchphrase for the next six months. Of course, she'd not told Mammy she was feeling better. Not yet anyway. It was her only way of staving off the aqua-jogging.

Quinn put the bottle on the worktop and jogged over to the table. He was clad in his new tracksuit ensemble, ready for the morning's run he had planned with Tom. He planted a kiss on top of Aisling's head, resting his hands on her shoulders and giving them a gentle massage as if he were a boxing coach encouraging his protégé to get back in the ring. 'It's so good to see you enjoying your food again, Ash.'

Aisling mumbled something incoherently because of all the oats in her mouth, repeating it once she'd swallowed. 'You make the best porridge.'

'Don't let Mammy hear you say that.' Moira looked over from the sofa where she was trying to wrest a non-compliant Kiera into a chunky green cardigan. 'Any chance of a bowl, Quinn?'

'There's some left in the pot. Help yourself.' He began doing hamstring stretches and Aisling looked at him, wondering if his look-alike Ronan Keating went jogging. If so, would Ronan wear electric blue velour? She wasn't sure about that or the velour but Quinn had assured her his choice of Adidas Challenger athleisure wear was very much the go this year. Aisling was in no position to argue, given her burnt orange outfit. Still and all, it could have been worse. He could have taken up cycling and been gadding about in those teeny-weeny bike shorts like cut-off male ballerina tights.

Her thoughts strayed to ballet. Mammy referenced her heavy footedness at the Howth boutique when she bought the sari dress because ballet hadn't come naturally to her. The salsa dancing was much more her thing, and she was back enjoying the Tuesday night dance sessions with Quinn at Lonzano's dance studio now she was feeling better.

The three sisters all had ballet lessons at some point, but Roisin was the only one who hadn't resembled a baby elephant thudding about in a leotard and pale pink slippers. Her eldest sister was the most graceful O'Mara girl and the bendiest thanks to her yoga.

Aisling remembered the glassy-eyed look Mammy would get when Roisin did her recitals and had known she was envisaging talking about her eldest daughter, a celebrated ballerina in the Irish ballet, to anyone who'd listen.

Poor Mammy had been crushed when Rosi announced she was more interested in boys than ballet, and she didn't have time for both. So, in a desperate attempt to stop her from ditching the dance, Mammy bought exorbitantly priced tickets for herself and her girls to see *Sleeping Beauty* performed by the Russian ballet.

Patrick flounced off to his bedroom in a strop at being excluded from the outing and had only come out when Daddy promised to take him to the greyhound racing as a special boys' outing.

Aisling reckoned he'd have much preferred the ballet and thinking about it now, she could see it was terribly sexist behaviour on her parents' part. However, the *Billy Elliot* film, which came out the year before, meant they were much more enlightened about boys and the ballet these days.

'Do you remember when we got in trouble with Mammy at the ballet?' Aisling tossed over at Moira, her mouth twitching at the memory.

'Where did that come from?' Quinn asked, swapping his hamstring stretches to the sort of lunges that would have made his mammy-in-law proud. It was lucky for him she'd yet to invent a Mo-pant for men.

Moira set Kiera down on the floor and began packing the baby bag. The little girl made straight for Uncle Quinn. He was like a magnet to her when he was in the velour, Aisling had noticed. It must be the texture of the fabric because Kiera was going through a tactile phase at the moment. She watched as her husband stopped lunging and whisked his niece up, making her giggle by swinging her up in the air and then pretending to drop her.

'When you used your outdoor voice in an indoor setting,' Moira said, smirking. 'Of course, I remember.'

Aisling giggled and put on a child's voice. 'Mammy, why's that man after putting a sock down his tights like Pat does when he's pretending he's Superman?'

Quinn paused in his tossing of the babby to laugh. 'You didn't?'

'She did.' Moira began to laugh. 'Jaysus wept, the way yer man came tiptoeing out on the stage like with the—'

'Bulge in his ballet tights,' Aisling finished for her, and they both dissolved into fits.

'Mammy told you it was the last time she brought you to the ballet because you'd behaved uncouthly, and the ballet was for cultured little girls,' Moira choked out. 'And she wouldn't buy you an ice cream at intermission.'

Aisling stopped laughing. That part hadn't been funny.

Moira zipped up the baby bag and got up. She made for the kitchen and began scraping the remains of the porridge pot into a bowl.

'Leave me some!' Aisling called, hearing the spoon scraping against the stainless steel bottom of the pan. There were traces of panic in her voice at the thought of being deprived of seconds. 'I am eating for three, you know.'

'It's not the magic fecking porridge pot,' Moira griped, toying with the idea of taking the last few spoonfuls. Aisling had a maniacal gleam in her eyes when it came to food at the moment, though and she wasn't game to take her on, so she dropped the spoon with a sigh. Lisa had said she'd make muffins for morning tea so she wouldn't go hungry, and carrying her meagre bowl over to the table, she sat opposite her sister. 'Pass the sugar.'

'Please.'

'*Please.*'

'Ready, mate?' Tom jogged into the living room dressed similarly to Quinn, except his tracksuit was a cross between forest and pea green.

Tom rocked most clothes he wore, be it his waiting attire or his trainee doctor's coat, and when he added a stethoscope, well, there weren't many women who wouldn't swoon, but Moira was not sold on the green velour. She watched as he grinned at his daughter, who was giggling, quite possibly at the state of her father and Uncle Quinn, as he launched into a round of stretches.

Meanwhile, Aisling was wondering whose big idea had it been for the two men to take up jogging in the first place. She cast about for the answer, settling on Donal of all people. He'd been a jogger once. A long time ago, when his girls were little and, given it would have been in the sixties, his tracksuit had probably been psychedelic polyester. He'd told Tom and Quinn that men needed 'me time' too when the babbies came along, and he'd found jogging therapeutic. Quinn's babbies hadn't come along yet, but he was embracing 'me time' whole-heartedly, as was Tom.

'Yep, good to go.' Quinn carried Kiera over to the playpen erected in the living room corner and gently placed her among her hordes of toys. She squealed and looked set to cry but was sidetracked by something bright made of plastic.

Aisling looked up from her bowl long enough to wave them off. 'Don't overdo it, boys.' The last thing she needed was for Quinn to pull something vital when he was supposed to be doting on her as the mother-to-be of his twins.

Tom let go of his flexed foot and obliged Moira, who'd angled her head for a kiss. 'Say hi to the Da Vinci girls for me,' he said.

'Ha-ha, very funny.' Tom found it amusing that the friends Moira had made at a mother-baby group she'd gone to in the early days after Kiera was born were called Mona and Lisa. The mother-baby group hadn't stuck, but Mona and Lisa had. 'I'm looking forward to catching up on all the news,' she informed her other half. It had been three weeks since they'd last got together, which was a long time in a baby's life. She was sure she'd see many changes in little Tallulah and Eva as Mona and Lisa would Kiera. 'It's good for Kiera to be around other babies,' she said, thinking it was good for her to be around other mammy's too, apart from when her daughter decided to snatch the Bob the Builder hammer off Eva. There had been a tense few seconds as Lisa waited for her to explain to Kiera that snatching was not okay. Kiera had given her mammy a look that hinted at the teenager she would one day become as Moira took the toy off her.

It could have been worse, Moira mused. Kiera could have bopped Eva over the head with the toy hammer like she had Pooh with the xylophone mallet.

'Jaysus wept, the state of them,' she said once the front door closed. 'You realise it will be the Dublin Marathon they'll be making noises about entering next, don't you?'

'Oh, I don't think Quinn's that serious. It's just a bit of keep fit fun is all,' Aisling replied airily, getting up to check Moira hadn't cleared the porridge pot out. She'd all but licked it clean when she returned to the table.

'That's what Lisa thought too when her husband Matt bought the velour athleisure wear and began jogging around the block. I'm telling you, Ash, it starts innocently enough. A few kilometres here and a few there. Then before you know it, they permanently reek of wintergreen, and you do too because they're forever after getting you to massage their calves. Things have already amped up a notch just like Lisa said they would because they've progressed from around the block to the Phoenix Park or Grand Canal loop paths. The next stage is the marathon. They'll come home looking pleased with themselves because they're after putting their names down for it any day now, and we'll know we're really in trouble.'

Aisling stared over the table at her sister, knowing she'd regret asking but needing to know the answer anyway. 'Why?'

'The riding rations, that's why. The marathon menfolk get all precious about needing early nights and how they've to conserve their energy on account of all the fluids they'll be losing when they attempt their twenty-six miles. They can't afford to lose anymore, you see.'

Alarm saw Aisling's spoon clatter down in her bowl. Quinn had been on the riding rations since the morning sickness had set in. The horse had only just been let back out of the stable. She couldn't have him running a marathon. Moira hadn't finished yet either.

'Oh, and there's something else you need to know as the wife of a marathon man, Ash.'

'I'm not the wife of a marathon man. I'm not.' Aisling picked up her spoon and began furiously scooping up the porridge.

'As I said, it's only a matter of time I'm sad to say. For both of us.' Moira shook her head, her dark hair swishing back and forth, and Aisling momentarily forgot about marathon men as she remembered her empty bottle of salon-only shampoo. Before she could demand compensation, Moira had begun speaking in a conspiratorial whisper that saw Aisling lean over the table to hear better what she was saying.

'Okay, this is very, very important, Ash. Be sure to tell Quinn to wash his hands before he goes for a wee if he's been at the Deep Heat. Otherwise, he'll be feeling the burn where there should be no burn.'

'Christ on a bike, Moira. I'm trying to enjoy my breakfast here,' Aisling spluttered, sitting back. Poor Tom, that wouldn't have been pleasant, she thought, shuddering before telling her sister, 'Would you feck off away to your friends and leave me in peace.'

'I'm just saying is all. Tom said he wouldn't wish the burn on his worst enemy.' Moira got up from the table and carried her bowl over to the sink, not bothering to rinse it as she left it on the worktop and disappeared to her bedroom.

She reappeared five minutes later, looking suspiciously taller than she had moments earlier, and it wasn't down to Cathal Carrick's hidden support either.

'Lift the hem of your jeans,' Aisling demanded, glowering at the black leather toes protruding from her sister's bootlegged bottoms. She was kneeling by the playpen, waving Postman Pat at her niece. She'd been telling Kiera that just because Postman Pat was male didn't mean girls couldn't be posties. 'You've got my Louboutin's on, haven't you?'

Moira neither confirmed nor denied this. Instead, she moved like the wind, swooping her daughter up and out of the playpen. Then, slinging the baby bag over her shoulder and picking up her car keys, she legged it out of the door with Kiera dangling from her hip, thinking it was a great joke; all before Aisling could haul herself up.

Chapter Eighteen

♥

A few mornings after the dire marathon man warning, Aisling sifted through the pile of envelopes on the table, her eyes locked on a plain white one. She picked it up. It didn't look like a bill, and turning it over, she gave a sharp breath, registering the sender's name.

It was from Sara Scott.

She pulled a chair out and sat down, almost frightened to open it. Christmas was approaching like a freight train, and with the guesthouse being at full capacity, she'd all but forgotten about Sara Scott's stay. Freya had put her mind at ease that Bronagh's oversight had been smoothed over, and when it came down to it, she'd no proof the woman even was a hotel inspector. All she had was a feeling, and feelings could be wrong. Now though, here was proof her suspicions about their Northern Irish guest had been warranted.

There was no point sitting staring at it, and Aisling tore the envelope open with the same gusto Mammy used to rip the sticking plasters off. Inside was a slip of paper to which a paperclip attached a smaller handwritten top note. She scanned the message, reading how Sara Scott had been assigned to write a review, attached, of O'Mara's Guesthouse for the Irish edition of the travel guide publication she worked for. She went on to say she'd enjoyed her stay at O'Mara's and wanted to say a special thank you to Freya. The night receptionist was an asset to the guesthouse. She'd signed the note, Sara.

Aisling put it to one side, eager to be put out of her misery as she skimmed over the first part of the review.

O'Mara's had been rated ten out of ten for location. That wasn't a surprise. They were in a prime position across the road from St Stephen's Green with the Iveagh Gardens behind them and Grafton Street, one of Europe's busiest shopping streets, less than a five-minute walk away.

She frowned, seeing they'd been given an eight for their facilities because of the lack of a lift. That was fair enough. She'd felt it herself when she'd had a sore ankle, but the old building didn't lend itself to being able to install one. The closest thing they had was the dumbwaiter running from the downstairs dining room to the family apartment. Still, they could hardly stuff their guests inside the dumbwaiter to ferry them between floors. Her frown vanished, seeing a nine out of ten for value for money and being family-friendly.

It was good, and she sat back in her chair to digest it for a moment. Better than good. It was excellent, and she sought out the overall appraisal of the guesthouse at the bottom of the paper.

9/10

A graceful, Georgian guesthouse sympathetically refurbished in keeping with its heritage, O'Mara's offers treetop views over St Stephen's Green and bed and breakfast style accommodation in the heart of central Dublin.

Cosy and quaint, this boutique guesthouse is situated in a second-to-none location and harks back to a bygone era.

Tucked away downstairs is a dining room where you'll be treated to an all-inclusive breakfast, arguably the best full Irish on offer in Dublin. Either way, it will set you up for a busy day spent relaxing in the green spaces of St Stephen's Green, shopping on Grafton Street or sampling the delights of Dublin's entertainment district.

Whatever you decide to do during your visit to Dublin, it's all there on the doorstep, along with links to public transport across the city, including the Air Coach to Dublin Airport.

If you're looking for friendly, family-run accommodation with an authentic vibe and outstanding service, you'd be hard-pressed to find better than O'Mara's, the Guesthouse on the Green. Oh, and if you're lucky, you might even meet the red fox who likes to visit after hours.

Aisling punched the air three times for good measure and smiled at the reference to Mr Fox. She was grateful Sara Scott hadn't been privy to Mrs Flaherty's charming reaction to finding he'd been at the bins again!

'Why are you behaving like you're at a Bon Jovi concert, and Jon just started singing "Living on a Prayer"?'

'Jaysus, Moira! Don't sneak up on me like so. It's dangerous in my condition. What are you doing back? I thought you'd left for college.' Tom had dropped Kiera off at his mam's this morning as per their childcare arrangements.

'I had, but I got halfway down the road and realised I'd forgotten my portfolio.' Moira hovered there waiting for Aisling to explain what she was so excited about, obviously not in a hurry to get going.

Aisling picked the piece of paper up and held it out for Moira to see. 'Remember I told you we had an undercover hotel inspector staying with us?'

'How could I forget? You were a pain in the arse making sure everybody behaved.'

Aisling flapped the paper at her. 'Well, this is why; read it.'

Moira stalked over and, taking the review from her sister, she skimmed through it, handing it back to Aisling with a grin. 'That's grand. You'd best ring Mammy and tell her. She'll be delighted with that, so she will. I love that Foxy Loxy got a mention.'

'I know. It's a grand Christmas present, so it is. It's Freya we've got to thank for this.' Aisling was already thinking of a generous Christmas bonus for their newest staff member.

'Isn't it you who's always after saying it takes a team to run O'Mara's? I can't find a 'T' for team in Freya.'

Aisling nodded. 'I know, but listen to this.' She picked up the note and read it out. When she'd finished, she looked at Moira and said, 'See, yer woman says it herself, she's an asset. She'll get a chance to prove herself when she steps in while Bronagh's away too.'

'There's something about her, Ash.'

'Moira, we've had a chat about it not being fair to lump her in with Emer.'

Moira shook her dark hair and frowned. 'No, it's more than that.'

'It's all in your head because she's proving indispensable to O'Mara's.' Aisling considered confiding her worries regarding Bronagh to her sister. Perhaps then she'd understand why she thought so highly of Freya. The younger woman had come to the rescue on more than one occasion since she'd begun work at the guesthouse. Moira being Moira, though, would insist on tackling Bronagh about what was going on, and Aisling didn't want her thinking she'd been discussing her behind her back. So, she said nothing, not even when Moira added.

'Nobody's indispensable, Ash, you know that.'

Chapter Nineteen

Freya plucked the chair from the kitchen table, saying a brief hello to Johan, the burly South African who shared the room opposite hers with his Australian girlfriend, Tracy. He was frying onions, and a packet of mince and a jar of pasta sauce were set out on the worktop alongside him. Usually, the whiff of onions cooking upset her, not the smell because she didn't find it offensive but rather the way it transported her back to the long-awaited family holiday she'd had such high hopes for.

Tonight she wouldn't let anything trample on her good spirits and leaving Johan to it, Freya dragged the chair out to the cavernous hall. She placed it down on the chipped lino next to the shelf on which the phone sat.

The old, red brick house in Rathmines had three chimneys and boarded-up Victorian tiled fireplaces with each room as draughty as the next.

It was a faded beauty serving as a house share for Freya and five others from various walks of life.

Freya would have liked to have befriended her housemates but barely saw them, given her days were spent at the DIT and evenings at O'Mara's. Then when the weekend came, no one was ever home.

The door to the living room was ajar and Tracy lay sprawled on the sofa with a cigarette dangling from her fingers. The house was fully furnished, and the couch had seen better days with its sagging middle. Tracy was adamant the cigarette burn on the arm had been there when she and Johan moved in but looking at her now, Freya wasn't so sure. It wouldn't be coming out of her deposit, that was for sure. She didn't smoke, but the smell of cigarette smoke didn't bother her because her mam used to smoke.

The blonde girl looked up and waved at Freya before turning her attention back to the *Friends* episode she was watching. Freya held a hand up in acknowledgement before pulling the door shut. If she'd known Tracy better, she'd have barrelled into the living room, blocking her housemate's view of the television to share what a good day she'd had.

Her mood was upbeat thanks to Aisling's effusive praise for how she'd handled the hotel inspector, Sara Scott. It was thanks to her quick thinking they'd received five stars.

Freya might even have poured her and Tracy a wine to celebrate. Johan always had a bottle of red lying about and he wouldn't mind them cracking it open.

Perhaps she'd get to know the couple now tech was closed over Christmas, and she was pulling an eight to four shift at the guesthouse thanks to Bronagh officially being on leave.

She sat down, crossed her legs, and wiggled her woolly sock-clad feet. She needed to tell someone. Keva perhaps? She bit her lip thinking about her pretty younger sister. She'd taken off to London on her twentieth birthday six months ago, convinced a glittering career in modelling awaited her, but she hadn't banked on the heavy competition. To date, she'd been booked for one catalogue shoot. Her savings had dwindled rapidly in the expensive capital and she'd had to top up the wage she earned temping for a call centre, but then she'd met Rupert.

Freya had seen a photograph of him, and he looked like a Rupert or what Mam would have called a Hooray Henry. He did something that earned him shedloads on the share market and was more than happy to foot Keva's bills so long as she played the role of arm candy correctly and didn't voice her opinions.

Keva had taken umbrage when Freya told her she needed to stand on her own two feet and not rely on some rich fella because she was not Julia Roberts in *Pretty Woman*.

Keva was out then and her brother Joey, a car salesman a year older than herself, was only interested in himself. She couldn't be bothered listening to him drone on about his bodybuilding protein diet to squeeze what she had rung to tell him in between hearing about the muscle-building properties of tuna, eggs, and whey powder. He looked like a nightclub bouncer these days with his bulging biceps.

Freya picked up the phone and stared at it. She wasn't close with her siblings, and this was down to Mam, who'd been quick to herd them off into the world as soon as they turned eighteen, equipped with little more than a nose for survival, a trait inherited from her. They'd scattered in different directions once they were no longer her financial responsibility, keeping in touch at a distance. Their father, too, had been relieved his maintenance payments could now cease. It was hard for a man to support two families.

He wasn't a bad man. He wasn't even a selfish man, ticking the boxes as he did each year for their birthdays and Christmas. Her father was, however, emotionally absent from the lives of his children from his first marriage. As a result, a distance had grown between them as the years passed.

He'd made a concerted effort to see them regularly when he and Mam separated but eventually, her bitterness had rubbed off on the three siblings, though unlike the other two, Freya knew her mam had no right to that bitterness. That was a secret she'd never shared though.

Her reasons for keeping her father at arm's length were different and complicated to articulate even to herself.

The best explanation she'd come up with was that she'd caught him looking at her over something said or done over the years and had known he was wondering whether she'd turn out like his ex-wife. This hurt because she wasn't sneaky or selfish like her mam. So she wouldn't be phoning him either.

She supposed she could telephone Martina. But unfortunately, there'd been a definite cooling of that friendship when she stopped working at Boots and no longer had a staff discount to purchase her friend's cosmetics.

A disconnected feeling settled over Freya, loneliness, and she shivered inside her sweater. She prided herself on not needing anyone.

'I don't need you. I don't need anybody!' Emer Lynch had flung at her husband when he left. Although given her reliance on Great Aunt Nono's goodwill, to say she didn't need anyone wasn't the truth.

Freya didn't like to think she needed her mam, but she found herself tapping out the number of Great Aunt Nono's Claredoncally cottage.

It rang five times.

'Hello, Noreen Grady's residence. Emer Lynch speaking.' Emer had kept her married name.

'How're you, Mam? It's Freya. I'm ringing to tell you how I'm getting on at O'Mara's.'

'Freya. What have I done to deserve this? Are your brother and sister still alive? Because I've not heard a peep from them in months either. And I left messages with both of them about Christmas dinner.' There was an accusatory tone in her voice.

As her mam wittered on about the ingratitude of children, it was like a slow puncture had pierced Freya's previously buoyant mood because it wasn't a chip so much her mam carted about on her shoulder but rather a boulder.

'What about Christmas, Mam?' Freya finally managed to squeeze in.

'Yes, well, I was going to ring you about that. But, I'm assuming since I've not heard, your brother's too caught up with his girlfriend to bother coming to see his mam, and as for Keva, she always was a daddy's girl.' Emer sniffed, knowing Freya didn't get on well with her father's new wife and wouldn't opt to spend her Christmas with her eejit ex, Martin, and whatever her name was. 'I can count on you, though, can't I?'

Freya had no desire to get the bus down to Claredoncally for Christmas so that she could feel like a third wheel while her mam and Great Aunt Noreen shared inside jokes. Mam was right insomuch as Keva would opt to spend Christmas with their dad and his wife Patricia as she did most years. Freya couldn't speak for Joey, though.

'Aunty Nono and I can't be bothered with the faff of cooking Christmas dinner this year and are thinking of booking a table at a local hotel instead. So I'll book it for three, shall I?'

Freya thought fast, and then it came to her. 'Mam, I'm going to be working at O'Mara's on Christmas Day.' She was surprised she'd not thought of it earlier. It hadn't crossed her mind who would be working Christmas Day. She supposed it fell to Aisling to man the front desk if she couldn't find cover. By volunteering her services, she'd have the perfect excuse not to traipse down to Claredoncally and make herself that little bit more indispensable in her employer's eyes.

'Working?' Emer sounded like she'd never heard of the concept.

'Well, somebody has to be out the front to see to guests, Mam. The guesthouse doesn't close just because it's Christmas.'

'Why can't Aisling or Moira cover for you.'

'Last on board always draws the short straw, Mam.' Freya laughed, making light of it for her man and wishing she'd let it go.

'Well, I think it's terrible you have to work.'

Freya would have loved to have said, 'We can't all sponge off rich widowed aunts now, can we?' But she managed to hold her tongue. As her mam prattled on, the smell of onions got stronger, and Freya's eyes smarted as though she'd been the one chopping them as she was swept back to that long-ago family holiday.

Chapter Twenty

♥

Freya, 1991

'Mam, Joey keeps breathing on me, and his breath stinks of egg,' eight-year-old Keva griped from where she was sandwiched between her older siblings, Freya and Joey. 'It's making me feel sick.' She screwed her face up to emphasise her point. Keva didn't like car journeys to the Tesco, let alone this nearly two-hour trip they were an hour into. Dad had insisted on taking the scenic route instead of the motorway, and it hadn't gone well with Mam or Keva.

It was typical Keva because Freya was getting hit in the face with her pigtail each time she swung her head round to try and see out the window but was she moaning? No, she was not. And, yes, Joey's breath did stink of eggs thanks to the sandwiches Mam had passed over when Dad had stopped to fill the car up at the Texaco. The whole car reeked of eggs, but nobody else was making a fuss.

Freya had harboured a secret hope that they might stop for a picnic lunch on the way down to the mysterious Curracloe beach of their daddy's childhood. She'd imagined herself, Keva and Joey sitting cross-legged on a tartan picnic rug with a babbling stream nearby. Each had a wedge of ham and egg pie and a glass of fizzy lemonade to wash it down. Mam and

Dad, meanwhile, were seated on the brand new fold-out camp chairs, enjoying their pie and the view with a mug of tea from the thermos. There would be sponge cake for afters and not a single piece of fruit in sight, although strawberries would be alright. So she amended her daydream to include sponge cake *and* strawberries.

That's all it was, though, a daydream, because Mam wasn't the pack a picnic type. She was the type who'd buy sandwiches and two Galaxy bars from the petrol station to be shared amongst them. There was no thermos, but a bottle of fizz had been passed about, which caused Joey to burp and Keva to kick off.

Mercifully, Joey couldn't hear his little sister thanks to the earphones he had stuffed in his ears, and the tinny thud of Vanilla Ice resonated from his portable CD player, a generous present from Nana and Grandad to thank him for mowing their lawns when he went to stay with them in Claredoncally.

If Freya had known there was a CD player in it, she'd have been vying for the job. As it was, she'd told Nana Roz the last time they'd visited that she was next in line when Joey retired.

Her brother would have given Keva a dead arm if he had overheard her complaining about him and World War III would have erupted. Freya was desperate to avoid this because she didn't want anything to spoil their first proper family holiday. So she jabbed her sister in her side with her elbow and mouthed, 'Shut up.'

Keva predictably opened her mouth to tell on her, but Freya gave her such a menacing look she thought twice and folded her arms across her chest, slumping in her seat.

Usually, they piled in on top of Mam's parents for a week each July. Dad didn't come because someone had to stay behind to run the family's furniture business. There wasn't much in Claredoncally, no swimming pool or beach, but they didn't mind because Granddad Terry would play board games with them, and Nana Roz taught them to bake. They got to run wild in the surrounding countryside, and the woman in the corner shop always gave them extra sweets when they called in with the holiday spends Dad had given them.

She always looked at them oddly, too, and when Freya mentioned this to Mam, she'd said she'd far too much imagination for her own good. It was a mystery, just like the whispered words between Nana Roz and their mam about how now she was home, she should try and make amends with Noreen. Who was Noreen? Freya had wondered, but she'd never got to the bottom of it.

The best thing about their week in Claredoncally was how the frown embedded between Mam's brows would soften. She'd look younger and happier than she did when they were at home. Freya thought it was because she didn't have to cook or do housework, and she wished her dad was there to see how pretty Mam looked.

Nana Roz would say, 'Put your feet up, Emer. You work hard, love, in that business of yours and Martin's. Sure, you deserve a break.'

Dad worked hard, too, and he didn't get to put his feet up, so this seemed unfair to Freya.

Freya gazed out of the window at the fields streaking by, thinking there were lots of mysteries when you were a child. Like why they didn't have the sort of holidays her classmates did. They either spent time by the sea here in Ireland or went abroad.

Mam and Dad had a furniture shop business because Mam had a background in furniture, and Dad was a good salesman. Freya didn't like to be disloyal, but she couldn't help but think they mustn't run Lynch's Family Furniture very well. Otherwise, Mam wouldn't always complain to Dad about having no money because the business was sucking them dry. However, this year was different because they were camping in Curracloe. It was thanks to Granddad Lynch, who'd passed away three months before, leaving Dad his worldly goods, which

Mam said hadn't amounted to much. Freya couldn't have been more excited if he had left them a fortune.

The boot of the family car was loaded with things like sleeping bags, pillows, towels, camp stretchers, a tent, a cooler box and a new set of camping chairs.

Dad had wanted to bring his fishing rod, but Mam had put her foot down because they could only fit the rod in by sliding it through the middle of the seats, and she'd no wish to wind up with a hook in her cheek; thank you very much. He hadn't pushed it, and Freya had thought about saying he could use her fishing net but had decided it probably wouldn't be the same.

Her dad might not have pushed the fishing rod, but he had been determined they go camping. He didn't often put his foot down, but the only reason they were going on holiday was because of the money he'd been left, along with the tent and paraphernalia that went along with it.

Mam would have liked an all-inclusive week in Spain, but Dad wanted Joey, Freya and Keva to experience the joys of camping in Curracloe like he had when he was a child. Golden days they were, he'd say wistfully. In the end, she'd only agreed to go on the condition the children sleep in the tent while they hired a static caravan for the week.

Freya had caught shouted snippets of furiously whispered words about deserving better when she was supposed to be asleep. Her parents fought a lot about money or the lack of it.

Mam would be fine once they'd arrived and unpacked, Freya thought as she stopped gritting her teeth, satisfied there'd be no more out of Keva. She could unfold her green camping chair, and once she opened the book she'd had beside the bed forever, she'd unwind.

Freya couldn't wait to sink her feet into hot sand and then cool them off in the sea. She planned on starting a shell collection and exploring the wet sand for crabs when the tide was out too. But, most of all, she wanted to roast marshmallows on a campfire under a starry sky like the little girl in her favourite childhood storybook had.

The countryside was whizzing by in various shades of green. Freya wondered whether she should instigate a game of eye spy. That was the sort of thing you did when you were on a car trip. Joey wouldn't play, obviously, but Mam, Dad and Keva would surely be up for a game. She took the plunge. 'Eye spy with my little eye, something beginning with P.'

'Person!' Keva shrieked.

'No, and he's a farmer, not a person. F, you eejit.'

'I'm not an eejit. You are!'

'Keva, don't bellow in our ears like so.' Emer looked back over her shoulder, displeased.

Freya willed her mam to join in and get into the spirit of it all. 'C'mon, Mam, have a guess.'

There was a huffy sigh from the front passenger seat, and Freya saw Dad shoot his wife an amused glance. 'Do you need a clue, Emer? Is that it?' he asked.

'Powerlines,' she said, ignoring him.

'No.' Freya shook her head. 'Dad?'

'Let me see, P. Peat!'

Emer began massaging her temples.

Freya laughed. 'No.'

'We give up.' Keva lisped.

'Potatoes.'

'Potatoes?' three outraged voices chimed. 'Where?'

'In the fields over there.'

'That's not a potato patch,' Emer said. 'It's sugar beet.'

Keva threw up.

Emer shot her husband a look that said Keva throwing up was all his fault and seeing the exchange made Freya feel sick. Then her dad pulled over on a grass verge, and Mam and Keva got out of the car. Keva was in tears as Mam swiped at her shorts with a handful of tissues, and then worst of all, Freya thought, was Mam getting in the back with her and Joey.

Meanwhile, Keva lorded it over them in the front because she said she didn't feel sick up there.

The remainder of the journey had passed in silence apart from Mam's occasional sigh that said she'd known this was how it would go and the muted music of Vanilla Ice. Things couldn't get much worse, Freya thought.

She was wrong.

Chapter Twenty-one

♥

'Where are the chairs? Emer demanded, her head in the boot of the car. All the important things were unpacked now and the tent was pitched on the grassy site but not without difficulty mind and her husband's irritating happy camper spirit had deserted him as he tried to figure out what pole went where in the canvas monstrosity.

Emer could have happily told him exactly where the poles should go but had bitten her tongue, fearful the tent would be abandoned in favour of them all squishing into the caravan, which was barely big enough to swing a cat in as it was.

Joey's stint in the scouts stood them in good stead, thank goodness, and once he'd wrested the poles from his dad, he'd soon had the tent up.

'I packed them. They should be in there, Emer,' Martin replied from where he was driving the final peg into the ground, determined to have some input in erecting the tent.

'Well, they're not there now.' Emer straightened up and sent him an accusatory glare. 'I asked you twice if you'd packed the chairs and you said yes. We bought them, especially for this week. So what are we supposed to sit on now?'

'Well, I'm sure I packed them.' Martin straightened and went to inspect the boot for himself, but there was nothing left besides a cricket set and fishing nets.

Freya, who'd just returned from the shower block having changed into her swimsuit, stopped brushing the sand off her feet and watched as her mam folded her arms across her chest and said something to her dad, which she didn't need to hear to know was unkind. Then her mam wrenched the caravan door open, clambering inside before slamming it shut behind her.

The pale blue aluminium tiny house seemed to radiate animosity on the site opposite the tent.

'Don't worry, Dad,' Keva, sitting cross-legged on the grass nibbling on a biscuit she'd found somewhere, lisped. 'There's room in our tent.'

Freya and her siblings left their dad knocking on the caravan's door, pleading with Emer to let him in, in favour of the beach.

'Keep an eye on Keva,' Martin called after them.

'I will,' Freya promised as Joey took off ahead of his sisters.

'Do you think Mam will let Dad back in the caravan?' Keva asked as they reached the sandy strand separated by waving beach grass that would lead them down the vast strip of beach.

'Of course, she will.' Freya assured her sister. Not because she was confident Mam would get over the chairs having been forgotten but because it was a big sister's job to reassure her little sister. 'Race you to the water. The last one in is a rotten egg!'

Keva squealed, 'That's not fair! You're taller than me.' They charged towards the shimmering blue water.

By the time they returned to the campsite, shivering inside their towels with sand coating their feet, the smell of burgers frying was wafting tantalisingly over from the barbeque area.

Freya dropped her handful of shells outside their tent and waved back at her dad, who clutched a pair of tongs. Her eyes flitted to the nearby picnic table where her mam was sipping from a plastic tumbler as though nothing had happened.

Freya quickly absorbed the open bottle of wine, a two-litre bottle of Tango, a plate of plump buns, cheese slices, a bowl of lettuce with salad servers protruding from it and a bottle of tomato sauce on the table in front of her. The Tango soft drink was a treat because Joey always got silly on the orange fizz chasing his sisters about so he could slap them on the cheeks and say, 'You know when you've been Tango'd,' in a deep voice like the orange man in the Tango television ad.

The knot between her shoulders loosened because her mam's foul mood had been blown away by the fresh sea air. Everything would be alright after all.

'Go and wash that sand off youse in the showers,' Emer called out as she reached for the wine bottle.

Fifteen minutes later, their togs hung dripping from the communal washing line after lukewarm showers. They'd all changed into warm tops and trousers for the evening ahead. It was a lovely feeling being clean and snuggly inside her clothes after catching waves all afternoon, Freya thought, bunching up on the wooden seat, eager to assemble her burger.

The mood around the table was upbeat, with Joey not even being told not to talk with his mouth full as he announced this was the best burger he'd ever tasted. 'It's even better than Eddie Rockets,' he declared, giving them a good look at the chewed-up burger patty. Freya didn't even find it annoying when he asked her to pass the ketchup instead of the tomato sauce as though he was an American.

'You're to gather twigs from the woods over there.' Martin pointed to the copse at the far edge of the campground. 'For the campfire, we'll build on the beach later.'

'Are we going to toast marshmallows over it?' Please let there be marshmallows; Freya's fists were clenched under the table with her nails digging into her palms as she waited for the answer.

'We are.'

'Yay, marshmallows for pudding!' Keva got up and did a dance that made them all laugh. 'I bags the pink ones.'

'G'won with youse. I'll run these through.' Emer said, gathering up the plates.

The wine was putting Mam in a very good mood, Freya thought, following Joey's lead towards the trees.

They carted armfuls of spindly, dry twigs, grasses and shards of bark down to the beach where the sky was streaked pink and purple, piling them up on top of one another before running back for another load. As they charged past the picnic table where their parents were seated, Martin called out, 'That will do.' He lowered the can he'd halfway to his mouth. 'It's a campfire we're after having. Not a bonfire.'

He followed them back down to the beach where the waves created a rhythmic shushing in the background. 'We'll build a fire like a teepee,' he instructed, and crouching down and grabbing a handful of the dried grass, he balled it up for the base. Joey dropped to his knees, helping him while Freya and Keva selected twigs to skewer their marshmallows.

As Martin announced the fire was ready, Emer appeared at the entrance of the strip of sand leading to the beach with an enormous bag of marshmallows. 'You can do the honours, Joey.' He handed him a box of matches.

Joey's eyes lit up, and he struck the match against the strike strip, holding the flaming stick to a ball of kindling. As the fire took hold, they all jostled for the marshmallows, eager to thread them onto their sticks.

'Poke it down the bottom, like this,' Emer demonstrated before pulling her stick back to inspect the browned marshmallow. She blew on it and, pulling it off, popped it in her mouth.

'What's it like, Mam?' Keva was jumping about with excitement.

'Stop waving your stick about Keva. You nearly got me in the eye then,' Martin exclaimed. 'Joey, if you poke that in much further, you'll lose it.'

'Delicious,' Emer proclaimed.

Freya's marshmallow was nearly black and bubbling when she pulled the stick from the fire burning her fingers in her eagerness to taste it. The exterior was crunchy and middle sweet and gooey. It was quite possibly the yummiest thing she'd ever eaten. She paused to look at her family before plucking another marshmallow from the bag. Their faces were orange and happy in the firelight, and Freya realised this was the most perfect moment in all her twelve years.

Chapter Twenty-two

♥

On their second day at the camping ground, a big, shiny wagon towing a modern caravan rolled in just as they finished gritty ham sandwiches.

The sand got everywhere, Freya thought, shifting on the wooden bench to pull her togs out from her bum. From the picnic table, they all watched the drawn-out, complicated reversing attempts into the empty site next to their mam and dad's caravan until finally, their dad took it upon himself to go over and help. He reminded Freya of the gardai officer she'd seen directing cars when the traffic lights had been out at the intersection near school a few weeks back. At last the caravan was inched into place and a family tumbled forth from the car.

'Thanks a million,' the man wearing a white polo shirt with shorts said, holding his hand out to shake their dad's. At the same time, the woman pushed her enormous tortoiseshell sunglasses on top of her head and smiled at the curious Lynch family before introducing herself. 'We're the Ryans from Cork. I'm Elaine, and this is my husband, Pat. Our children Kieran and Siobhan.'

Freya tried not to cringe as her mam put on that voice she always used when meeting new people and returned the introductions. Joey, who had a breadcrumb stuck to his lip, began acting like an eejit at the sight of Siobhan with her flicky blonde hair.

'Teenagers,' Keva said, watching Joey and Siobhan's posturing interaction. She rolled her eyes in Freya's direction, making her laugh.

Kieran too was smirking. He was between Keva's and Freya's ages with spindly arms and legs. His glasses were thick, and squinting through them, the youngest Ryan sized the sisters up.

Freya guessed he was trying to work out whether they might hang about together for their stay. Then, as his mam told him off for scuffing the toe of his trainers against the sandy ground, and he pulled a face which made her and Keva laugh, she decided they'd get along just fine.

'That's an impressive caravan you've got there,' Martin said, not without a hint of envy in his voice.

Pat's chest expanded as he reeled off statistics like 1990 touring, Buccaneer Caribbean, four-berth and Elaine rolled her eyes at Emer mouthing, 'Men,' making her laugh before inviting her to have a look inside.

'We've only just bought it,' she said over her shoulder, stepping inside, Emer close behind her. 'We normally holiday abroad, but Pat, for whatever reason, decided we needed to experience the delights of an Irish summer and go caravanning. So we're here for a week before heading to the West Coast for another five days.'

Freya trailed in after them, listening to her mam's exclamations over all the mod cons contained within what was effectively a rather flash home on wheels. It defeated the purpose of camping, in Freya's opinion. If you wanted luxuries, you'd be better off going to a hotel in Spain. Which, she supposed, was exactly what her mam had wanted to do.

She received a sharp look, and knowing it annoyed her mam when she hung around the adults, she left them to it, not wanting to spoil the good humour she'd been in since yesterday afternoon.

Mr Ryan looked up from where he was unhitching the caravan from their car and smiled.

Freya smiled back. Mr and Mrs Ryan seemed nice even if they were a bit show-offy.

'Have you seen Keva?' she asked Joey, who was falling all over himself offering Siobhan an earphone so they could both listen to EMF's, 'Unbelievable'. He was such an eejit.

'She headed down to the beach with Kieran and Dad for a game of cricket.'

Freya, not wanting to miss out, hared down to join them.

The afternoon whizzed by with cricket on the beach and swimming, ice creams, and then at dinner, they shared the biggest lasagne Freya had ever seen with the Ryans. Mrs Ryan had brought it from home, and it tasted ten times better than Mam's. This was because she used jars of sauce, whereas Mrs Ryan told them hers was homemade. Freya had mopped up what was left of the delicious meal with a piece of garlic bread, earwigging on the adults' conversation—a habit that also annoyed her mam, but she was too engrossed in listening to Mr Ryan talking about the property business he and his wife ran to notice.

Freya didn't know what was involved in running a property business, but she figured the Ryans must be better at it than Mam and Dad were at the furniture business because they owned a caravan. She was fascinated by the posh voice Mam was putting on once more, and she tried to make herself invisible while the other kids mooched off.

'We needed to get away and spend time with the children,' Emer said. 'It's important to make time for the family, don't you think?'

'Yes, definitely,' was the murmured reply from across the table.

Dad wasn't saying very much, Freya noticed, scarpering before she got roped into doing the dishes.

That night the adults drank wine and beer while playing cards under the awning of the Ryans' caravan. Freya, Keva and Kieran played a boisterous game of hide-and-seek while Siobhan and Joey slunk off in the direction of the beach.

Freya found an excellent hidey-hole around the back of the communal kitchen behind the bins. She sat with her knees bunched under her chin, hearing Keva run past, looking for her a few minutes later. Time ticked by and she began to get cramp. Also, someone was frying onions in the kitchen, and the smell was drifting through the louvred windows. She suspected she'd reek of it by the time she was discovered. To distract herself while she waited for Keva to find her, she thought about the previous night toasting marshmallows around the fire on the beach and the way she'd felt like they were a proper family all together like that. Now though, they'd branched off in different directions, the caravan, the beach, the camping grounds and in her case, behind the bins!

'Freya, I give up!' Keva bellowed.

Pleased at having won, Freya unfolded herself and ran over to where Keva and Kieran were standing near the tent.

'Where were you?' Keva asked.

'Not telling.' It was too good a hiding place to give it away.

'Do you want to play swing ball?' Kieran asked.

'But there are only two bats,' Keva said.

'Well, I get to have a hit first because I won hide 'n' seek and obviously Kieran does too because it's his set. You can play whoever wins the first game.' Freya smiled sweetly at her sister, who looked as though she might protest for a second but then flopped down on the sandy grass to wait her turn.

Chapter

Twenty-three

♥

T hree glorious days of sunshine followed, with Martin announcing that this part of Ireland got the most sunlight in the country as though he was personally responsible.

All the Lynches were sporting sunburn of some description, with Freya resembling Rudolph the Red-Nosed Reindeer.

The two families had settled into an easy routine of lazy days spent by the beach and shared meals in the evening followed by games for the younger children, cards and drinks for the adults. As for Joey and Siobhan, it had become apparent what they were up to by the red mark on Siobhan's neck. It had seen Mr Ryan glowering at Joey, and their dad taking him aside for a man-to-man chat. Freya was desperate to listen in on that conversation but knew she'd be for it if she got caught. The outcome was there was to be no more disappearing down to the beach on their own at night.

Adults made silly rules sometimes, Freya thought because she'd seen them kissing the faces off each other around the side of the tent, hidden from their parents' line of sight.

Martin had appointed himself chef that evening, deciding hot dogs were on the menu. Camping, it would seem, had the bonus of no vegetables gracing their plates. However, the three Lynch children had argued the night before as to whether tomatoes counted. Freya was adamant they were a fruit, Joey a vegetable. He'd won because he was bigger.

So it was Freya, clutching a tub of margarine upon which two onions balanced, trailed after her dad who was loaded up with provisions, down to the communal kitchen. He'd asked her to give him a hand, and given she'd been waiting for a turn at swing ball, she'd obliged. If she were at home, she'd have moaned that it wasn't fair Keva and Joey didn't have to do anything but things were different when you were on holiday.

Another family was seated at one of the tables in the utilitarian kitchen, tucking into spaghetti Bolognese. A woman was heating baked beans in a pan on one of the cooktops.

'I'll get the barbeque hot, and you can chop the onions into rings for me, Freya,' Martin instructed.

Freya liked that he trusted her to use the sharp knife because Mam wouldn't let her at home. She wasn't enamoured with the onions because they were making her eyes were stream, but she stoically chopped them into circles as she'd been instructed.

Her dad returned to take the chopping board to the barbeque, and Mrs Ryan appeared as she was about to start buttering the bread. Her face had tanned in the days since they'd arrived at Curracloe and it suited her. The Ryans, annoyingly, all tanned instead of burning.

'I'll see to that, Freya. Things are getting tense over the swing ball. Perhaps you could go and suggest a game of hide 'n' seek instead? You're good at sorting the younger two out.' She dimpled at her and Freya stood a little straighter as she put the butter knife down and said she would.

As she ran past the barbeques, she saw her dad was in his element with a pair of tongs in one hand and a can of beer in the other. The onions she'd chopped were now heaped on the hotplate next to the sausages and gave off a tantalising aroma that made her mouth water. It seemed ages since they'd had their afternoon ice cream.

'The sausages are pink in the middle, Freya. Tell your mam we'll be eating in another fifteen or so minutes,' Martin called after his daughter.

'Will do,' Freya called back, and then her step faltered. 'Dad?'

He looked up from where he was turning the sausages and raised an eyebrow.

'I wish we could stay here forever.'

'Sure, you'd be sick of sausages after another week.' He clacked the tongs together making her laugh, and she carried on. If it meant staying in Curracloe forever, Freya reckoned sausages for dinner was a small price to pay. The sound of Vanilla Ice rapping led her over to the tent. Joey and Siobhan were stretched out next to each other in an intense conversation.

'Have you seen Mam?' she interrupted.

Joey shook his head but didn't look up. She heard a cry go up and rounded the tent in time to catch her little sister throwing her bat down like a bad-tempered Wimbledon player before stomping off.

'Hey, don't be like that, Keva. Let's play hide 'n' seek instead,' Freya called after her. She wanted to show Mrs Ryan she was capable of managing things. 'It's still another fifteen minutes until dinner.'

Her little sister turned around with a sulky expression, arms crossed firmly over her chest. 'Only if I don't have to be it.' She raised her chin, challenging Kieran to disagree.

'I'll be in,' he said. 'But that doesn't mean I was cheating.'

Freya popped her head inside her parents' caravan. There was no sign of Mam, but she smelled her perfume, and the book she'd been reading was splayed open on the table in a way that would have Miss Winters, the school librarian, in fits.

'Have you seen Mam?' Freya asked, closing the door. Keva shook her head.

'I'll count to thirty,' Kieran said, putting his hands over his eyes and, her mam forgotten about, Freya took off. She'd already decided to use her secret spot behind the bins again.

There was no one about, and rounding the corner of the kitchen block, she ducked into her hidey-hole. In such close quarters, she realised she'd not washed her hands after chopping the onions, and they reeked. All she could smell was onion. She breathed through her mouth and, hearing someone moving about inside the kitchen, listened out, wondering if it was Kieran trying to see if either of them was hiding in there.

Then she heard her mam's familiar tinkling laugh. She shifted about, careful not to knock the bins and peeped through the cracks.

At first, she couldn't see her, but then she saw movement towards the woodland where they'd collected the kindling for the fire the other night. It was her mam's yellow top that had caught her eye. She strained to see what she was doing and realised she wasn't alone. Mr Ryan was with her. They must be collecting twigs, although she hadn't heard anyone mention another fire on the beach. There was something strange in the way they were standing so close together though and then Freya saw them spring apart as her dad strode towards them. He was shouting something, but she couldn't catch what it was. Mr Ryan took a step back, and Freya stared in disbelief as her easy-going father swung at him. Her mam was clinging to her dad's arm, shouting something, but she was too far away to catch it.

The ground beneath Freya no longer felt solid and she pushed at the bins, eager to get away before it swallowed her whole. The lids clattered to the ground, and she clambered to her feet, registering Mrs Ryan was now making her way towards the three adults beside the trees. She turned away, running past Kieran, who shouted, 'I found you!' She kept running until her feet connected with the sand.

It was still warm but no longer felt soft on her feet. Instead, it was gritty. Freya stumbled blindly over to the waving grasses and sank into them, covering her face with her hands. She knew she'd never toast marshmallows with her family again, and sobbing into her hands, all she could smell was onions.

Now

Freya realised her mam had moved on from the topic of Christmas and was asking her a question.

'Sorry, Mam.'

'I asked what it was you were ringing for.'

'Oh, nothing important. Listen, I've got to run.'

'Before you go, there's something else.'

What now? Freya wondered.

'Aunty Nono is making noises about a family reunion next summer. Do you think you'll be able to make sure you're not working for that?'

Freya rubbed the spot above her right eye that had begun to ache. She could think of nothing worse than a family re-union and she'd not missed her mam's dripping sarcasm. 'That sounds like a great idea. Tell her from me, Mam. I've got to run. One of my housemates wants to use the phone. I'll give you a call Christmas Day.' She put the phone down. No one was waiting to use the phone. She felt keyed up with her insides twisted and her earlier euphoria a memory.

Her mam always made her feel like this because it was always there. The memory of what she'd done in Curracloe. Freya could not let it go. Worst of all was how she'd pleaded with their dad by saying her dalliance with Mr Ryan hadn't meant anything. Why had she done it if it meant nothing because Freya's life was torn into segments after that holiday?

Their family hadn't been perfect before that disastrous week, but they'd been a solid unit. After the holiday, they'd splintered, leaving too many jagged pieces to put back together again.

Chapter
Twenty-four

♥

'There it is, the car park of doom,' Moira said, flicking her indicator on and turning in.

The sudden ringing of Aisling's mobile jolted her out of her trance as they stared at the squat building Moira was driving towards.

'Is it Mammy?' Moira asked.

'Who else?' Aisling replied, holding her mobile like a hot potato. 'What should I do?'

'Don't answer it.' Moira's hazel eyes were beseeching while Aisling's widened, registering the car backing out in front of them. The blaring horn saw Moira slam her foot down on the brake, causing both sisters to lurch forward and back in their seats.

'Jaysus, Moira! Pay attention to what you're doing. You've a pregnant woman in your car.'

'It's Mammy's fault for distracting me,' Moira said, glaring back at the woman pulling out of a parking space in front of them. 'And the stupid woman wasn't looking where she was going.' She tapped the steering wheel impatiently. 'It's me who has the right of way.'

Technically accurate, Aisling thought, massaging her neck, but Moira hadn't been paying any attention to what was in front of her, so she didn't blame yer woman there for glowering. She realised the phone had stopped ringing and was about to stuff it back in her bag when it began jangling away merrily again.

'Listen,' Moira said, nosing the car into the just-vacated space and coming to a halt halfway in. 'Don't answer it. She doesn't need to know we're here.'

'I bet you she knows already. She's got eyes everywhere.'

True, Moira thought, idling the car. She was unwilling to turn the engine off, not while there was still a chance of escape. 'It's not too late, Ash. Just say the word, and I'll hit reverse. We could leave this place for dust and go to a nice warm café for a cuppa and something sweet to eat instead. What do you think?' Her hand hovered over the gearstick, and she gunned the engine to show her sister she was serious.

'You've no idea how much I would love to do that.' Aisling exhaled as the phone stopped ringing. She tore her eyes away from the building in front of them. It was so nondescript it was positively menacing. She gave Moira a wistful glance. 'It'd be pointless, though, because she'd only make us come back another day. There's no getting out of it, Moira. You know that. Sure, we're better to get it over with.' They were united in their solidarity of the awfulness of what Mammy was making them do, and she almost took hold of her sister's hand but decided that would be overkill. 'I promise we'll be okay if we stick to our plan.'

Maureen had cottoned on to Aisling's morning sickness being no more when she'd caught her with her hand in the good biscuits tin the last time she and Quinn called over. Aisling had been on her third chocolate digestive when she'd felt eyes drilling into her back. There'd been no denying it, not when she'd chocolate crumbs down her front, and half a digestive jammed in her gob.

Mammy had wasted no time ringing Rosemary Farrell, who'd booked them into this place.

It was a place Moira and Aisling had no business being.

The Aquatic Centre.

'Right. Yeah. The plan. Run it by me again.' Moira edged the car in and turned the key in the engine. As the car stopped, she twisted to face her sister.

Aisling retrieved her swim bag from down by her feet and holding it tight against her like a talisman, said, 'Okay, listen carefully. First, you're to complete a full length of the pool, and then as you're halfway through your second lap, cry out that you've hurt your knee. Then, put on a real show and me, being the caring, more considerate older sister, will tell Mammy there's no need for her to leave her friend. Sure I'll take you to the doctor. That's when we make our escape but don't forget to hobble as you leave the pool, or she'll be after us.'

'Can't you do the injury? You're the more dramatic one,' Moira said, reaching over into the back seat for her swim bag. 'Sure, you'd make a better job of it. Look at the performance you put on with your foot.'

'What performance? I was stoic, so I was. And besides, you're the better actress. I never get away with anything.'

Moira wasn't sure whether to take this as a compliment or not.

'G'won practise. Do the agonising pain face again,' Aisling urged.

Moira rolled her eyes back in her head and opened her mouth in a grimace as she flapped her hands manically.

'What's with the hands? That wasn't in the script.'

'I'm flailing in the water.'

'Oh, very good. Improvisation. I like it. Listen, Moira, you've got this. Oh, for feck's sake!' Her phone rang again, and jabbing at the button, Aisling held it to her ear and demanded, 'What?'

'Aisling O'Mara, that's no way to speak to your mammy!'

'O'Mara-Moran, Mammy. Moira and I are now on our way into the Aquatic Centre.'

'Well, I'm very glad to hear it, so I am because Rosemary and I might be retired, young lady, but that doesn't mean your time is more important than ours. We're busy people, I'll have you know, and you were supposed to be here ten minutes ago. You'll find us in the foyer.'

The line went dead and Aisling shoved her phone back into her handbag. 'C'mon. She's on the warpath. We'd best get a move on.'

Aisling set off while Moira locked the car, and then waited by the entrance for her to catch up. 'Remember the plan,' she said before pushing open the glass doors. Moira nodded.

The sisters were hit by the eye-watering smell of chlorine and muffled shrieks of small children in the pool beyond the glassed-in wall. Maureen was upon them before they'd had a chance to close the door. Rosemary was right behind her, staring meaningfully at her watch. 'Glad you could make it, girls,' she said with a decent dollop of sarcasm.

'I've already paid and put Kiera's name down for the swimming lessons. You can't start them too young, you know, Moira. We live on an island after all.' Maureen didn't wait for a reply as she herded them both through to the changing rooms. 'I hope you bought flip-flops with you because you don't want to be catching the verrucas. Roisin had a dreadful one the size of a fifty pence piece when she was doing the swimming lessons as a child, Rosemary. You've got to be so careful.'

The two women, who'd had the foresight to wear their swimsuits under their clothes, stripped off while having a hearty discussion about the removal methods for plantar warts.

'Did you bring flip-flops?' Moira whispered to Aisling, tipping her towel and swimsuit out of the bag and onto the wooden bench.

'No.'

'Feck, me neither. I don't want a verruca.'

'It's not on my wish list either. Leave your trainers on. And don't worry, we'll be out of here before you know it.'

'I hope you bought the sensible swimwear like I told you to,' Maureen said, waiting with a towel wrapped around her. 'Do you need a hand there, Rosemary?' She frowned, watching her friend struggle with a bright yellow swim cap.

'No, you're grand, Maureen,' Rosemary said, one eye pressed flat by her silicone cap, giving her the look of Quasimodo in a no-nonsense navy swimsuit.

Aisling, her red togs in her hand, turned to her mammy, on the defence. 'I wasn't going to buy a special swimsuit to go aqua-jogging in Mammy. Quinn and I are starting a family, you know. We've other priorities.'

'Me neither,' Moira added, pulling her sweatshirt over her head. 'I've other priorities too.'

'I'm aware of that, but it's a public pool, girls. That means there's likely to be elderly menfolk with heart troubles doing laps as I speak. Now, if you two go waltzing out the changing room with the bits of string up your bottoms, it could see the poor fellows off. Do you want to be responsible for that?'

'No.'

'Listen, they've the lovely hire swimsuits out the front. Why don't I get you both one?'

Aisling and Moira looked at one another in horror. If you could catch a verruca off the changing room floor of the Aquatic Centre, what could you catch from a pair of hire togs? Besides, they were bound to be hideously unflattering.

'No, Mammy. Sure, it's our own swimsuits or nothing,' Aisling stated dramatically.

'I think you'll find swimwear is required,' Rosemary interjected. 'If it's the nude swimming you're after, you'll have to go to Donabate near Malahide there. Although, you'd want to be careful because your bits could fall off in this weather.'

Aisling didn't want to dwell on how Rosemary knew about such a place, and she'd had enough of standing here in the stuffy changing rooms in her bra. 'Listen, do you want us to join you out there in the pool or not because Moira and I can turn around and leave right now if you're going to make a fuss about our swimsuits.'

Moira nodded her agreement emphatically, wishing Mammy would make an almighty fuss so they could leave.

'She's getting very bold now she's with babbies, so she is Rosemary,' Maureen said, not rising to the bait as she turned to her friend, who was still struggling with the swimming cap. 'Come on. We'll wait for them out there.' She flounced out of the changing room with her flip-flops flapping, Rosemary clicking and clacking behind her.

Aisling and Moira hastily got into their togs and bagged up their clothes before exiting into the pool area with trepidation. A vigorous aquarobics session was underway down the far end with the instructor striking the poses to Madonna's 'Vogue' song blaring out from her boom box.

'I feel stupid,' Moira said, glancing down at her trainers. 'I look like I should be doing the aerobics, only I've forgotten to put my tights on under my leotard.'

'You look like you've the tights on with all that St Tropez you're after slapping on.' Aisling eyed her sister's bronzed legs before gazing down at her lily-white legs and special shoes. She wished she'd had the foresight to fake tan. 'Is it water-resistant?' Aisling asked as they plodded over to where a mammy was keeping an eye on her little ones splashing in the toddler pool.

'I don't know. I hope so. Otherwise, I'll be going in one colour and getting out another.'

'Jaysus, would you look at the state of Rosemary,' Aisling whispered as they made their way over to where the two older women were in conversation with a lanky, lean lifeguard standing beside the racks of equipment.

'She looks like a bright yellow condom with that thing pulled down over her head. Do you think she wears it to the nudist beach?' Moira said, making Aisling giggle.

'And what's with the goggles? I didn't think we were putting our heads under. The chlorine always makes my highlights turn green,' Aisling said in alarm. She'd piled her hair high on her head, but she drew the line at the swim cap.

Neither of them was aware of the poor auld fella who'd come up for air as he did the freestyle and had caught sight of two nearly bare bums undulating past the slow lane. He'd swallowed water and begun having a coughing fit. Meanwhile, the short, stout lifeguard in the orange top and red shorts was blowing her whistle to try to distract her colleague who was closest to the man but was otherwise engaged demonstrating the flotation belt to Maureen and Rosemary.

The old man managed to doggy paddle over to the side, and the drama was over by the time the lean, lanky lifeguard with the flotation belt realised what was happening. He resumed his laps and the small crowd who'd gathered to watch dispersed.

Maureen, flotation belt over her black swimsuit with the special control panel Ciara had put her on to, was tight-lipped upon seeing her daughters approach.

Rosemary happily took charge by passing the sisters a belt each and showing them how to put them on with all the flourish of a flight attendant demonstrating how to activate the life jackets. Once they were kitted out, the foursome advanced to the pool edge.

'On your marks, get set—'

'Mammy! Stop it. It's not a race,' Aisling said, dipping a toe in the tepid water.

Rosemary had a glint in her eyes, however, and sitting down first, she dropped into the water. Maureen, who could sniff out a challenge like a beagle could a rabbit in a hole, entered the pool with a splash.

Aisling and Moira, who were after all their mammy's daughters, followed, and when Mammy shrieked, 'Go!' they were all off like the clappers, their arms pumping, their legs doing their best to fight against the pull of the water as they each focused on the unspoken finish line—the short, stout lifeguard's feet.

None of them made it.

Fifteen minutes later, they were all dressed, loitering in the car park, shooting looks at Moira that conveyed, It's all your fault.

'She didn't need to blow her whistle so hard,' Aisling griped.

'I haven't been manhandled like so since I set the sensors off in the airport shortly after I'd had my hip done,' Rosemary said. 'I might sue.'

'The shame of it. Being evicted from the Aquatic Centre,' Maureen lamented.

Moira put her hands on her hips. 'What I want to know is what the auld fella was doing swimming behind me like he was fecking Jaws going in for the kill in the first place. It's not my fault I elbowed him in the face. He was invading my personal space.'

'You gave him a bloody nose, Moira,' Aisling reminded her sister.

'Sure, it was only a trickle. So there was no need to evacuate the whole pool. It wasn't like when you did the wee, and the water changed colour.'

'Shut up, Moira.' Aisling had chosen to forget that incident. As far as she was concerned, it never happened. 'It was surprisingly fun, though. I wouldn't mind giving it another go.'

'Me too.'

'Well, you'll be going on your own. Sure, I can't take you two anywhere. C'mon, Rosemary, let's go and get a cup of coffee.'

Aisling and Moira watched them go and then, seeing a horde of annoyed aquarobic attendees piling out of the Aquatic Centre, decided it would be a good idea for them to hit the road too.

Chapter Twenty-five

♥

T he days were getting swallowed up in the lead-up to Christmas, Aisling thought as she pulled back the bed-covers and clambered between the cosy flannelette sheets. The fluffy bedding was one of winter's little treats, and with a satisfied smile, she snuggled down.

It was the same each year as the big day approached, with the guesthouse fully booked until the new year. She was glad she didn't have to trawl the shops for presents at this late stage, having had the foresight to begin early to beat the rush. Unlike half of their guests, who were a mix of Irish come to the big smoke to go shoulder to shoulder with the crowds and do their last-minute Christmas shopping. The rest of the rooms were filled by tourists eager to experience the yuletide season in Ireland's capital city. Dublin was turning it on for them too, she mused, thinking about the beautiful Christmas lights illuminating the city. It wasn't just the decorations, though, because the atmosphere on the streets was festive. People took the time to smile and wish each other well this time of year.

It was only a little after nine thirty, she saw, glancing at the alarm clock. The digits glowed brightly in the dark. Quinn wasn't due home until late, so she was opting for an early night. She'd soaked in the bath for nearly an hour, topping the water up each time it cooled off. The flagrant use of hot water was her treat for having the earache from Mammy, who'd rung her the moment the credits for *Fair City* had begun to roll. She'd drawn the short straw because Moira had been tending to Kiera. Her niece provided her younger sister with a handy excuse, Aisling had noticed. Then, resting her hand on her middle, she smiled. She'd have two wonderful excuses of her own in six months.

Mammy had been in fine form, harping on and on about what a sad state of affairs it was when only two of her children would be home for Christmas. Aisling did feel sorry for her because she'd made no secret of harbouring high hopes Patrick and Cindy might make a surprise announcement that they were flying back to his homeland for Christmas. She'd hoped too that Roisin might wriggle her way out of a Quealey family Christmas with her ex-husband and his mother. It wasn't to be though. You had to play fair regarding shared custody arrangements, and Patrick and Cindy were far too busy with their respective careers to squeeze in a week in Ireland. It would seem the female personal hygiene advertising world would wait for no woman. As for Pat, well, none of them was sure what pie he currently had his finger poked in.

At least she'd been able to appease Mammy with the news that she and Quinn would be joining them for Christmas dinner, Aisling thought, hearing the faint strains of the television from the living room. Moira wouldn't be far off bed herself. She thought back to how she'd interrupted Mammy's flow to say, 'I know it's short notice, but Freya's after volunteering to man the front desk on Christmas Day as she's not going home this year. She said she'd rather stay in Dublin. I didn't delve into it, but reading between the lines, I don't think she's much time for her mam.' She'd held the phone away from her ear as Mammy had lamented how sad it was Freya would spend her day alone. Still, when Aisling had told her it was either her and Quinn or Freya who'd be seated around her table enjoying the turkey, she'd rallied around with, We can always put a plate together for her.

Aisling had pulled a face at Moira who was mouthing, 'Freya's a fecky brown-noser.' She didn't care what Moira thought because Freya was proving to be a Godsend, and a leisurely and uninterrupted Christmas dinner was well worth the triple time she'd offered her. Moreover, Mrs Baicu had confirmed she was on board to see to the guests' breakfast on Christmas morning, which meant everything, touch wood, was under control. Aisling stretched an arm out from under the covers and tapped the top of the bedside drawers to be on the safe side.

Bronagh left Freya with a list of instructions the length of her arm, and their receptionist had officially been on holiday for two days. It had been touch and go as to whether she'd leave the guesthouse when four o'clock rolled around two days before. She was torn between her loyalty to O'Mara's and wanting to spend time with her beau, Leonard Walsh. Aisling had hugged her tight and told her to go and have a wonderful break because she'd earned it. 'You're not to think about O'Mara's at all over Christmas. Enjoy your time with Lennie, Joan and your mam, Bronagh,' she'd urged. Of course, she didn't add that she felt Bronagh needed a rest given her recent out-of-character spate of forgetfulness. Then, she'd all but pushed her out of the door. Not before ensuring Bronagh promised to bring Leonard in to say hello. Sure, she'd thought waving Bronagh off, she'd be good as new after a few weeks R & R. She had to be because Bronagh was as much a part of the guesthouse as she was, and she couldn't imagine her not being here each morning with her bowl of Special K cereal and a not-so-secret stash of custard creams.

As for Freya, she was taking her temporary new role in her stride, Aisling thought, stretching out in bed and luxuriating in a few starfishes. She initially enjoyed having the bed to herself, but the novelty swiftly wore off, and she'd wish Quinn would hurry up and get home. It was strange, though, being greeted by Freya and not Bronagh in the morning and not just because no custard creams were waiting to be snaffled! The stash had been cleared out. Aisling knew because she'd checked.

It was time to shelve all thoughts of the guesthouse, and closing her eyes, she let her mind drift off to a warm and cosy dream where she was holding her babies. Sometimes she could even imagine their weight in her arms, although she couldn't picture their faces. She was smiling as she teetered towards sleep when a sudden clattering saw her eyes fly open. Her heart pounded as she stared into the dark and the beats only slowed when she realised who the culprit was: Mr Fox. It had been a while between visits.

A soft tapping on her door and a chink of light appeared from the hallway as Moira opened it. 'Ash, are you awake?' she whispered.

Aisling propped herself up on an elbow. 'I am now. Thanks to Mr Fox.'

The door creaked as Moira opened it further and stepped into the room. She was still dressed, but Aisling caught a minty whiff which signified she'd been brushing her teeth in readiness for bed. 'Foxy Loxy's up to no good down in the courtyard.' She made her way over to the window.

'I guessed as much.' Aisling pulled herself upright and, pushing the covers aside, slid her feet into the slippers beside the bed, unable to resist joining her sister at the window. Her robe was on the chair where she'd slung it, and she wrapped it around herself before padding over to the window. 'Shall I open it a little so we can see down into the courtyard properly?' Moira was still whispering.

'G'won,' Aisling said, her voice sounding loud, although why Moira needed to whisper, she didn't know. Kiera, once asleep, slept through anything. She braced herself for the onslaught of chill air, huddling next to Moira. They both peeked below to the illuminated courtyard, breath warm against the frosty night. The little red fox had set the sensor light off on his suppertime quest.

'Hello, you,' Moira called out softly. The fox's pointy features gazed upwards, and his yellow eyes locked on the sisters briefly, but the lure of fine dining pulled his attention back to the bin. He'd already nosed the lid off and the scraps were his for the taking.

'I hope there's a tasty bit of sausage in there for him,' Aisling murmured.

'And some black pudding,' Moira added. 'White, too.'

'He loves bacon rind,' Aisling stated.

'Left-over toast triangles always go down well too,' Moira said knowingly.

'Mm, toast.'

'Aisling, you don't need toast.'

'No, but the babies do. They always need toast lately.'

They watched entranced as Mr Fox as Aisling referred to the guesthouse's nocturnal visitor from the Iveagh gardens beyond the brick wall, or Foxy Loxy, as Moira called him, pulled half a sausage out of the bin. He gobbled it down then licked his chops before seeing if seconds were on offer.

'Ash?'

'Yeh?'

'Do you think it's weird us all living under one roof?'

'What do you mean weird?'

'You know. A bit communal like the Moonies or something. I mean, most people don't live with their siblings once they settle down and start their own family.'

'Moira, we are nothing like the Moonies. For one thing, we're not a secretive cult, and I might not know much about communal living, but I'm fairly sure their mantra is to share everything. I don't share my shampoo or shoes with you, now do I?'

'No.'

'So there you ago. And for another thing, we're the O'Mara's. Since when have we ever been like most people?'

'That's true enough.' Moira's teeth flashed white in the dark as she grinned.

A rogue wave of hormonal sentiment washed over Aisling. 'Moira, I think Quinn and I are blessed to have been a daily part of Kiera's life since she was born. And I wouldn't change having been there for the three of you for the world.'

Moira rested her head briefly on her sister's shoulder. 'Me neither. Becoming a Mammy would have been scarier if you hadn't been here. It will be crowded when the twins come along, and Tom and I won't be able to afford to move out for at least another year.'

'This is your, Tom and Kiera's home as much as it is mine, Quinn and these two's.' Aisling meant every word of it, she realised and all her worries as to how they'd all muddle along under one roof vanished. They were family, and muddle along, they would. She patted her stomach, and Moira's hand came to rest on top of Aisling's.

'You wait until you start feeling them flip-flopping about the place. It will be any day now.'

'Don't say flip-flop, Moira. It makes me think of Donal.'

'Fair play. Do you think our children will peep out of the window when they're supposed to be sound asleep to spy on Foxy Loxy when they're older?'

'How long exactly do you and Tom plan on living here?'

Moira laughed. 'When we come to visit like.'

'That's alright then, and they're bound to. Especially when their big cousin Noah comes over from London to see them all.'

'I miss Noah and Rosi. I wish they were coming for Christmas.'

'Me too.'

'Do you think Mammy will pay for us to go to the Greek Islands or Hawaii for Pat and Cindy's wedding because if we're to be bridesmaids we have to be there?' Moira asked.

'I don't know.'

'I wonder if Cindy will do a Pamela Anderson and get married in her swimsuit?'

'Mammy would go mad if she did,' Aisling said. 'And what would we wear if she's in her togs?'

Moira shrugged. 'I don't know. Togs too, I suppose.'

'Well, I'm not wearing a swimsuit and having my photo taken after having had twins.'

'I thought you said Mammy would go mad if Cindy said she was wearing togs?'

'I did.'

'There you go. It won't be a problem. I know something that will be a problem, though,' Moira said.

'What?'

'Donal will be wearing the flip-flops again.'

'Ah no.'

'Kiera's not showed any signs of fungi foot-'n'-mouth or the like, thank goodness.'

'Jaysus! Would you look at the size of that bacon rind Mr Fox is after pulling after him.'

The little red fox stopped as he reached the hole under the brick wall and turned to look back up at the sisters.

Aisling waved down and Moira called out night-night. They watched him slink back through to the gardens on the other side before closing the window.

'Mm, bacon.'

'Aisling, you don't need anything else to eat.'

'I'm eating for three, you know. But alright, maybe I'll just have a slice or two of peanut butter on toast,' Aisling said, trotting out of the bedroom after her sister.

Chapter Twenty-six

'Aisling. It's me. Your mammy.'

'Morning, Mammy.' Aisling tensed, picking up on her peevish tone, the reason for which she would find out any second now. In the interim, she tried and failed to pinpoint anything she'd done in the twelve hours since they'd last spoken which might have annoyed her. Nor had Moira been up to much. However, she had taken the last slice of bread for her breakfast this morning. That had been annoying, not to mention selfish. When Aisling had confronted her, Moira had replied there would have been plenty of bread for breakfast if Aisling hadn't eaten three-quarters of a loaf before bed the night before. Aisling had informed her she was eating for three.

Her eyes flitted to the pantry. She was peckish right now but, hearing the heavy breathing down the phone, knew food would have to wait. Was it Roisin or Pat who'd upset Mammy then? She put down the red pen she'd been using to scribble 'paid' on the monthly invoices spread on the table and braced herself.

'I'm after hearing from your great aunt Noreen this morning.'

'Oh yes?' It was the festive season, Aisling supposed. Family reached out to one another this time of year, even if no one could ever offer a clear and concise explanation of how the

O'Mara's were related to Noreen, Emer, Freya and the rest of them who Aisling didn't think she'd ever met. 'That's nice.'

'No, it wasn't, Aisling,' Maureen snapped. 'She wasn't ringing to wish me and Donal well. Or for an update on how you're getting along and how Noah and the babby Kiera are doing. She was concerned about Freya.'

'Freya?' Aisling was puzzled. 'Why? Sure, she's grand. I saw her earlier this morning, and she's managing the front desk like she was born to it. I told Bronagh as much too when she rang to check in earlier this morning. Honestly, Mammy, the woman's supposed to be on holiday. I threatened to change the phone number on her.'

'It's grand Freya's working out so well, but Noreen and Emer are concerned that she felt pressured into working through Christmas, and I don't mind telling you, I didn't much care for Noreen's tone.'

'What?' Aisling was lost. What was she talking about? Pressured? There'd been no pressurising. She'd not got hold of Freya's arm and twisted it behind her back, insisting she work or else. Freya had volunteered.

'Pardon, Aisling. I didn't raise a heathen. And I think you heard me the first time.'

'But, Mammy, you know yourself, Freya put her hand up to work Christmas Day. She didn't want to go home for Christmas, and it's not entirely out of the goodness of her heart because she is being generously compensated.'

'I told Noreen that. Well, obviously, I didn't mention her not wanting to come home. I said she'd seemed perfectly happy to fill in at the guesthouse, and with her being a student, she probably felt the triple time you were paying her made it worth her while.'

'Exactly.'

'And I told them they needn't worry because Freya wouldn't miss out. I planned on sending you girls home with all the trimmings for her Christmas dinner and pud.'

'And what did Great Aunt Noreen say to that?'

'She said, be that as it may, Emer was terribly upset and felt Freya was getting taken advantage of because she was family, which wasn't on.'

Aisling felt her blood pressure begin to rise. 'Freya only got the job in the first case because we're related. Distantly might I add. I think I need to have a word with her.'

'I think that's a very good idea.'

Aisling was quick to finish the call. She was glad Moira had gone out for a walk with Kiera and hadn't been privy to her conversation because she wasn't in the mood for I told you so. As she headed out of the door, she nearly barrelled straight into a sweaty Quinn with an equally sweaty Tom behind him, and she stepped around them, giving them a wide berth.

'Great news, Aisling!' Quinn grinned, taking the hint and not homing in for a kiss.

'And what would that be?' It might restore her previous good humour. Okay, she'd been paying bills, so her humour had been average, but she'd settle for average.

'Tom and I are after putting our names down for the Dublin 2002 marathon. It's not until October, so we've ten months to get ourselves in the peak physical performance of our lives.'

Jaysus wept, would yer listen to him! Aisling thought as the reality that she was going to be married to a marathon man, just as Moira had predicted, hit home. Oh yes, she would be hearing I told you so when Moira returned from her walk, alright.

'Great news indeed, lads,' she said weakly, leaving them to it. One thing at a time, she thought. A chat with Quinn about not putting her on riding rations so he could achieve his peak physical whatever could wait until later. For now, the first item on her agenda was Freya Lynch.

—ele—

Freya was restocking brochures reading through them as she went. She'd decided it was good to familiarise herself with the various activities on offer in the city. Knowledge was power, or so the saying went, and she liked to know what she was talking about if the guests queried any of the offerings. Aisling had mentioned seeing if she could get her a freebie on the Viking Splash tour or a trip out to Glendalough in the new year. The tour companies were usually open to filling an empty seat if it meant there was a recommendation in it for them.

First thing that morning, a man who would have looked at home tending his flock rather than hosting a tour of the Republic had appeared, introducing himself as Ruaraidh. He'd come to collect the Adamores, a lovely couple on the trip of a lifetime from Nova Scotia, and as they'd waited for them to come downstairs, he'd wheezed off all the destinations on the tour's itinerary. Freya hadn't seen half of the places he'd mentioned. By the time he left with the excited Nova Scotians in tow, it was her who felt like the culchie. She'd made a vow to try and see more of the country, not that she'd have any holidays owing for a while.

The morning was flying by. First, she'd snipped the stems of the flowers decorating the reception desk after noticing a petal had fallen off one of the tulips. It was in the hope the bouquet would last until the next delivery, which would be later than usual with businesses closing down for the Christmas period. Once the flowers were back in pride of place, she'd filled the condiment baskets in the guests' lounge, and then, after having a word with Ita, she'd got a glow on pulling the furniture out. This was so Ita could vacuum under it properly, which she'd done ungraciously.

The poor skirtings had been worse for wear when O'Mara's director of housekeeping had finished making Freya aware she hadn't appreciated being told what to do by her. They were close in age and, in the pecking order of things, Ita may have worked at the guesthouse longer, but Freya was the acting head receptionist. So it was on her to ensure the downstairs area gleamed, and a thorough hoovering was overdue in the lounge.

This fortnight, while Bronagh was away, was her opportunity to show Aisling what an asset to O'Mara's she was and that meant not sitting idly about waiting for guests to come and go. There was plenty to be getting on with, and you couldn't please everybody. Ita would get over herself. So too would Mrs Flaherty, who'd been terse with her this morning when she'd asked if she could use the cooker hood in the kitchen from now on so reception didn't smell like an Irish fry-up all morning.

Freya was lost in thought with a glossy brochure advertising a tour of the Guinness factory in her hand when Aisling made her jump.

'Freya, have you got a moment, please?'

She put the brochure in its place on the stand and turned to face Aisling. 'Of course. Is everything alright?'

'Not really.' Aisling tucked her hair behind her ears, frowning. She could feel her skirt beginning to strain uncomfortably at the seams as she waited for Freya's attention. The burnt orange sari dress was beginning to feel like a good option.

Freya was puzzled as to why her boss sounded annoyed. Had Ita run upstairs to complain about her throwing her weight around? Surely asking the housekeeper to vacuum where there were obvious dust balls wasn't overstepping the mark? She moved from foot to foot, anxious to hear what Aisling had to say.

'I'm after hearing from my mammy this morning, Freya. Great Aunt Noreen has been on the telephone with her, and she wasn't pleased, I'm afraid. She and your mam seem to think I more or less bullied you into working over Christmas. I could be wrong, and I apologise if you felt obliged to cover, but I thought you volunteered. You seemed happy with the remuneration offered too or did I misread the situation?'

Freya's face paled, and instead of the excuses, Aisling was expecting she did something that took her by surprise and burst into noisy sobs. Unsure of what to do, Aisling took a step backwards. She hadn't meant to upset her, and a loud sniff galvanised her into putting an arm around the younger woman's shoulder so she could steer her over to the seat. 'It's not worth getting upset about, Freya,' she said gently, waiting until she'd sat down to fetch a wad of tissues. 'I'm sure it's a misunderstanding, is all.'

Freya took the tissues and gave her nose a good blow, hic-cupping. 'I'm sorry for making such a show of myself, Aisling.' She looked at her through watery eyes and swallowed hard. 'I should have made it clear to Mam that I'd chosen to work over Christmas, but I promise I didn't tell her I felt bullied into it. I did offer to cover, and I am happy with the money you're paying me. More than happy.' Balling the tissues in her hand, Freya plucked at non-existent lint on her trousers for a moment, choosing her words.

'I think Mam's taken umbrage because none of us are going home to see her this year. Keva's going to Dad's and I don't know what our Joey's up to. We're not a close-knit bunch like you and your sisters. You're lucky with your family.'

Aisling nodded. She might not always feel lucky, but she knew she was. Her head was tilted to one side as she waited for Freya to finish.

'I suppose it's easier for her to convince herself I had no choice but to work rather than face up to my not wanting to come home. But Great Aunt Nono's house isn't our home even if Mam's made it hers.' Freya paused to blow her nose again before continuing. 'And I hate Christmas. Mam always gets maudlin about her and dad having broken up and how different her life would have been if they hadn't divorced. The mad thing about it is they would never have split up if it wasn't for her. It was her who cheated on him, you know?'

Aisling didn't know but then why should she? Her side of the family didn't mix much with Emer; if it weren't for Great Aunt Noreen, they would never see her. She shook her head slightly. 'I'm sorry, Freya.'

'She only thinks about herself and what she wants. And she doesn't care who she hurts to get it.' Freya took a shuddering breath. 'I never want to be like her. Never!'

The phone interrupted her tirade.

'I'll get it.' Aisling patted the younger woman on the knee and got up. By the time she'd taken down the booking. Freya had composed herself once more and her reddened eyes were the only signs she'd been crying.

'I'll ring Mam this morning and put her straight, and I'll apologise to Maureen for the misunderstanding.'

'Ah, there's no need to ring my mammy. I'll speak to her.' Aisling's earlier pique had vanished; instead, she felt sorry for Freya because she couldn't imagine not wanting to spend Christmas with your family. 'Why don't you have a break and make yourself a nice brew. I can manage here.'

However, Freya wouldn't hear of it, and Aisling took herself back up the stairs.

'Good timing.' Quinn grinned, his hair wet from the shower. 'Maureen's on the phone.'

Aisling rolled her eyes and took the phone from her husband. 'I've spoken to Freya, Mammy, if that's what you're ringing about, and she'll put Emer and Great Aunt Noreen straight.'

'I'm not ringing about Freya.'

'Oh.'

'No, I'm ringing with a wonderful surprise.'

'Have you burned Donal's flip-flops?'

'Aisling, you're getting very like Moira of late. It must be the hormones.'

'C'mon, Mammy, put me out of my misery. What's the surprise?'

'Us!' Roisin and Noah chimed.

Chapter Twenty-seven

Christmas Day

'How much longer, Mammy? I'm so hungry I could eat the back door buttered!' Aisling called out, craning her neck hopefully in the direction of the kitchen. She'd already had her hand slapped for helping herself to a slice of the honey-glazed ham studded with cloves as it cooled on the bench. 'But I'm allowed to eat it hot, Mammy,' she'd wailed. It had fallen on unsympathetic ears as she was shooed from the kitchen with a flap of the tea towel.

Now it was the smell of the turkey lovingly wrapped in streaky bacon and stuffed with a lemon that was making her drool. It was comforting to see Mammy beavering away at the worktop with Roisin by her side, but no actual, proper food was being brought to the table, which was of concern. Roisin flashed her a reassuring smile, and Aisling shot one back. Rosi was currently her favourite sister, given she'd sneaked her a roast potato when Mammy had announced them done before wrapping tinfoil over the tray to keep them warm. She wondered if Rosi might see fit to smuggle a second roastie her way.

Roisin and Noah descending on them for Christmas had come about thanks to Colin and his mam coming down with the flu and cancelling Christmas. As soon as they'd taken to their beds, Roisin had got straight on to Ryan Air to see if they could accommodate one adult, a child and a family of gerbils on a last-minute flight to Dublin.

Mammy had already declared their surprise visit the best Christmas present she could have wished for. Naturally, Aisling was as happy to see her sister as the next woman, but given she and Quinn had forked out a small fortune for an Arpège gift set, she thought this remark a little on the nose.

Shay, thinking he wouldn't see Roisin and Noah until after Christmas when he visited London, had opted to go to Sligo to spend a few days with his dad's side of the family. He'd stayed for his lunch and was now en route back to Dublin with an ETA to see him join them at the table for a bowl of Christmas pud and trifle if he didn't mess about.

'Hold your horses, Aisling,' Maureen tossed over at her pregnant daughter. 'You'll not be fading away.'

'Not in that dress,' Moira sniggered, referencing her sister's burnt orange sari dress. She thought it was hilarious that Aisling was twinning with Mammy in this season's hottest colour trend. 'If you climbed up to the top of the Howth lighthouse, people would think it was operational again.'

Aisling glowered over at her. 'It's very comfortable, and I won't be the one complaining that my waistband's after cutting me in half when we've had second helpings of the pudding.'

'Peanut?' Donal waved a dish under Aisling's nose.

Aisling's hand reached out.

'Don't be offering her anymore of those, Donal. They'll bind her up something terrible. Quinn won't thank you for it tomorrow.' Maureen warned from the kitchen.

The dish was whipped away as fast as it had appeared. Aisling blinked. Had it been a mirage? She turned her attention back to Kiera, who was perched on her lap, and continued to rub her back in a slow circular motion. For once, her little body was still as she concentrated on bringing up her wind. It must be nice to be a babby, she mused. All you had to do was open your mouth, and food or drink was crammed in.

The storm cushions had been hefted down the side of the sofa to make room for Moira, who'd been careful not to spill a drop of her seemingly bottomless glass of Baileys as she sat down. Thanks to Donal's superb hosting skills, drinks had been continuously topped up since they arrived. Aisling wished he was as free and easy with the peanuts.

A light snow was falling outside. It wasn't enough to settle on the ground, but still and all, there'd been excited squeals at the sight of it. Aisling felt like she was in one of the kitschy snow globes watching it, and she knew from experience that later when they were all stuffed to the brim, the warmth from the gas fire keeping the room toasty would make them drowsy.

Right now, though, Noah, sprawled out on the carpet in the middle of the room, was on high alert as he played a robust game of Mousetrap with his Uncle Tom and Quinn. Quinn was surprisingly competitive, Aisling thought, catching the intense concentration on his face as he plotted his move. She reached up and toyed with the heart pendant on the necklace she'd unwrapped earlier. It was beautiful, but the sentiment on the card enclosed in the jewellery box had made her cry. 'Because you're my heart.'

Her gift wasn't quite so romantic, but Quinn's face had lit up at the runner's kit she'd put together. She and Moira had gone out together and made up gift baskets of electrolyte drink tablets, more electrolyte drink tablets, blister-resist socks, no-tie shoe laces and whatever else they'd thought related to endurance running. Between them, they'd decided there was no beating their partners' new interest, so for the sake of the riding, the best thing they could do was ensure adequate fluid replacement.

Kiera's eruption startled them all, and Noah burst into giggles at his cousin's audacity.

'Clever girl,' Aisling said, popping her down on the floor so she could annoy Pooh. The poodle was on his bed, tuckered out from the heat and the doggy treats that had come his way earlier.

'We'll be serving the starter in five minutes,' Roisin announced, wiping her hands on a pinny as she joined them in the living room; Mammy had pulled it out of the bottom drawer and insisted she put it on so as not to mark her pretty dress.

Roisin was looking well, Aisling thought, although she was disappointed there was no sign of another illicit roast potato coming her way.

'What are we having?' Moira asked.

'Melon salad,' Aisling supplied. Mammy had taken her aside earlier when she'd barely had a chance to hang her coat up to break the news there'd be no smoked salmon starter this year. 'You're not to make a scene, Aisling, because I know it's your favourite, but I'm after reading it can give pregnant women the tapeworm.' She didn't repeat this to Moira, who'd already moved on.

'Are we phoning Pat and Cindy after dinner?' Moira's questioning gaze stayed on Roisin.

'Yes, it's scheduled in between charades and pudding.'

'Ah, not charades.' Moira groaned. 'Mammy always gets carried away. Remember the year she put her back out miming the digging for *The Shawshank Redemption*?'

'She does get right into her character. I love a good game of charades though.' Roisin said.

'Only because you always win,' Moira rebutted.

Roisin grinned. It was true. 'Squish up,' she said before squeezing between her sisters. She put her hand on Aisling's tummy.

'Don't press down too hard. You'll make me need to wee again,' Aisling bossed.

'I can't believe there are two little babbies in there.'

'A little Moira and Tom Junior.'

'Feck off, Moira.'

'Have you thought of any names?' Roisin asked.

'No. We haven't moved past the jelly beans. Speaking of which, Noah, can I pretty please have one of your jelly beans?' Her nephew having a big container of Haribo jelly beans hadn't escaped her notice when they'd been amid the present unwrapping frenzy earlier. A rubbish sack full of Christmas wrapping remained as evidence in the hallway.

Noah slid the container across the floor towards her. 'Don't take the purple, yellow, green, blue, black, white or orange ones, Aunty Aisling, because they're my favourites.'

In other words, she could have a pink one. Before she could help herself, the container was whisked out of reach.

'The starter is served,' Mammy announced, stalking to the kitchen and putting the jelly bean tub on top of the fridge.

'The table looks gorgeous, Mammy,' Roisin said, admiring the quilted Christmas cloth. 'Did you make this?'

'I did, and I have to say Roisin, the Christmas tree pattern is much more tasteful than the Father Christmas one Rosemary was after cobbling together.'

'What about this?' Roisin asked, and all eyes swivelled to the elaborate pine cone and holly centrepiece.

'My handiwork,' Maureen tittered, placing a glass bowl filled with green and pink melon cubes down at one of the place settings.'

'And did you fold the serviettes into stars too, Mammy?'

'For feck's sake, it's like watching a *Blue Peter* Christmas Day special,' Moira muttered, slotting Kiera into her high chair. Her special occasion Beatrix Potter bowl was placed in front of her, and she immediately picked up a melon cube and squeezed it in her fist before trying to find her mouth.

Maureen directed them to their seats while Donal ensured all glasses were full. Meanwhile, Noah wrapped two pieces of melon in his serviette, undoing half an hour's intricate folding in a split second as he slunk off to the guest room. He thought Mr Nibbles, Stef and the baby gerbils deserved a Christmas treat too, and passed the sweet fruit through the cage door.

'Noah, there'll be murder if you let them out,' Maureen's voice bellowed. 'And you'll not see yer jelly beans again.'

'Sorry,' he whispered to the gerbil family, ensuring the door to the cage was secure. 'I love jelly beans.'

He returned to the table in time to catch his mam extolling the virtues of gerbils as pets. He knew she was hoping to be a few gerbils lighter on the return trip, but no one looked impressed.

'Right, before we start, Donal would like to say a few words.' Maureen sat down and pursed her lips in Aisling's direction. Aisling reluctantly lowered the fork upon which a piece of melon was already speared and halfway to her mouth.

Donal put the empty bottle of wine down and picked up his glass, smiling at the faces dotted around the table before sending in a wink in Aisling's direction. 'I won't waffle on. I promise.' He angled his glass towards Maureen. 'Mo, thank you for this wonderful meal we're about to enjoy.'

A chorus of Thanks came from everyone. Aisling picked up her fork and then put it back down as Donal continued.

'Roisin and Noah, you've no idea how delighted we are to have you here with us today.'

'And Mr Nibbles, Stef and the babies,' Noah butted in, making them all laugh.

'And the gerbils, of course. My cup runneth over the day I met Mo, and you all came into my life.' He looked at each face around the table.

Maureen's face glowed as she beamed up at Donal.

'Donal, I'm eating for three, remember,' Aisling interrupted.

'And just think this time next year, there'll be two more babbies joining us at the table.'

Quinn reached over and placed his hand on Aisling's belly. She rested her hand on top of his.

'May peace and plenty be the first to lift the latch on your door, and may happiness be guided to your home by the candle of Christmas. Beannachtaí na Nollag duit!'

'May the blessings of Christmas be with you!' was echoed around the table, followed by clinking glasses.

Roisin was about to admonish Noah for being too enthusiastic and slopping his lemonade when Aisling's sudden gasp saw all eyes on her.

'I felt them.' Her green eyes were luminous. 'It was like tiny butterfly wings beating.'

'Like bubbles popping,' Roisin added, smiling at Noah.

'A tiny pulse,' Moira gazed at Kiera.

Maureen blinked back tears as she looked at her daughters. Two mothers already and one soon to be. Donal reached for her hand under the table and squeezed it. She was truly blessed.

Chapter Twenty-eight

Two months later

A isling was rifling through the rack in the lingerie department of Brown Thomas, looking at the range of maternity bras on offer. She'd nipped out shortly after four when Freya took over the front desk, and despite the lateness of the afternoon, the store was busy. She didn't want to spend too much on new underwear. Not when her belly and boobs were growing at a rate of knots. She'd only been in the non-underwire one she was presently spilling out of for a few weeks.

While she was here, she'd look at the maternity tops too, she decided, glancing down at her burnt orange go-to. It would be good to change things up a bit. Oh, and she'd need a new swimsuit too, now she and Moira were doing the aqua-jogging once a week. Leila and Moira's pal, Andrea, had joined them, and they'd all agreed it was great fun racing one another up and down the pool. Mammy and Rosemary Farrell refused to have any part of it.

Christmas was a memory now as Aisling moved into her fifth month of pregnancy. The horrid morning sickness and lack of energy were long gone and her libido had returned with a vengeance. Poor Quinn barely got a moment's peace, and the fluid replacement drinks she'd bought him for Christmas were already in need of replenishing. She'd confided in Moira with a lurid wink there was something to be said about men and marathons when it came to building the stamina. Moira had put both hands over her ears and pulled a face. Then she'd made some smart-arse remark about making the most of it because her stallion would be put out to pasture once the babies came.

The consultant she and Quinn were under informed Aisling that she'd entered the honeymoon period of pregnancy and to enjoy it. Their jelly beans were the size of grapefruit now, and she'd a gorgeous big round bump to prove it. They were active too, and she loved nothing more than grabbing hold of Quinn's hand when they were lying in bed so he could feel a foot or elbow as they jostled about.

She was relishing finally looking pregnant. People were so nice to you when you were pregnant, she mused, pulling a peachy-coloured bra out for inspection. They made way for you when you walked down the street and held doors open. Women you'd never met before started conversations asking when you were due. She'd even stopped traffic with a flash of her tummy at the oncoming cars. It was all so lovely. She gave a happy sigh.

As the months progressed, the more real impending parenthood seemed, and she and Quinn had begun pouring over the baby names book every chance they got. Initially, they'd found agreeing on girls' names challenging because she'd never realised how many girlfriends Quinn had before they met at college. Thus far, he'd never gone out with a Niamh or Aoife, and as for boys' names, the leading contenders were Connor and Finley. Moira was still pushing for Moira and

Tom Junior. Mammy had been pumping for Daniel after her favourite film star, Daniel Day-Lewis and Danielle for a girl. Donal was partial to Donny and Marie, while Roisin thought Kyla and Kennedy were lovely. The latter two were lovely but do it for one, they'd have to do it for all and would wind up with babies with ridiculously long names like Kyla Marie Danielle Moira Junior O'Mara-Moran. As such, all suggestions had been vetoed.

Aisling checked the size of the bra. She really could do with asking one of the assistants to measure her but was still haunted by her teenage exposé and would settle for carting an assortment of sizes bigger than the last one she'd bought off to the fitting rooms. She was bound to hit the jackpot with one of them, she thought, deciding the peach was pretty. Her phone rang before she could pluck any more bras off the rack and dipping into her bag for it, she saw it was a call from O'Mara's.

'Hello?'

'Aisling, it's Freya. I'm so sorry to bother you, and I won't keep you, but I've Mr Gibson from Room 3 with me, and he's after wanting to book himself and the family on a Viking boat tour. I remembered you saying you'd been on one and wondered which company you'd recommend.'

Aisling flashed back to her nightmare experience at the hands of a red-headed Dubliner. He'd refused to answer to anything other than Erik the Viking. No, she'd not be recommending Erik to the Gibsons. 'The splashdown tours are very good.'

'Grand, thanks, Aisling. Enjoy your afternoon.'

'No bother at all.'

Aisling put her phone away. She was also feeling much more relaxed about O'Mara's now she'd lessened her load by asking Freya to step in and help with the management side of things for the foreseeable future. The idea had come to her when she and Quinn had propped themselves up on their elbows in bed one night, both unable to sleep, and had a heart-to-heart about how they would navigate the guesthouse, the restaurant and being the best parents they could be.

Aisling realised the answer had been under her nose all along in a lightbulb illuminating moment. Freya had proved herself capable and able to use initiative while Bronagh had been away. She'd also touched on the financial side of hotel management as part of her course curriculum. So it made sense to offer her a promotion. She would still keep the same four until ten pm hours because they worked around college, but she'd have the additional responsibilities of managing budgets, controlling expenditure and ensuring they reached revenue targets. For, of course, extra pay.

Bronagh, who'd returned from her holiday full of vim and vigour, was in full favour when Aisling had broached the idea with her. She had been quietly concerned about how Aisling would continue as she had been when she became a mammy without assistance. It had also been a worry to her that Aisling might want her to increase her load, which with her mam to care for wasn't possible.

Yes, it had all worked out wonderfully because Freya had been beside herself with excitement, and Aisling had begun showing her the ropes. She was pleased with how quickly she was picking things up.

'Aisling, isn't it?'

Aisling's reverie was interrupted, and she swung around clutching the peach bras to see a woman she didn't recognise with a pram in front of her. There was something about her, Aisling thought. She was vaguely familiar, but for the life of her, she couldn't think how they knew one another. As the woman waited expectantly for her reply, her face heated up. This was awkward. 'Uh, yes.'

'I thought so. We met briefly a while back now. Well, two and a half months ago, to be precise, in the waiting room of the ultrasound clinic. Jodie Trimball? She gestured to her belly, 'Only I looked a little different.'

'Of course, we did! Sorry, Jodie, my brain's not much cop these days. It's lovely to see you again.' Aisling angled in for a glimpse of the swaddled baby in the pram. 'Who's this then?'

'Justin. He's just turned two and a half months. And I won't lie, it's been hard, but look at him.' Jodie smiled. There were dark circles under her eyes, but the pride in her son was evident on her face.

Aisling looked up from the pram and smiled back at her. 'He's gorgeous, so he is. I can't wait to meet these two.'

'Two?'

'Yes, I found out we're expecting twins the day we met.'

'Oh, how wonderful!'

There was an awkward pause before Aisling blurted. 'Would you like to go and have that cuppa now?'

'I'd love that, but it might be a little late in the day.'

Aisling glanced at her watch and saw it was four thirty. 'I've an idea. Hugh Browns upstairs will be open. We could have a cheeky little mocktail? What do you think?'

'I think I like your style, Aisling, and maybe share a bowl of chips?'

'You're a woman after my own heart.'

'But what about those?' Jodie indicated the bras Aisling had hold of.

'Sure, they can wait.' She hung them back on the rack and then she and Jodie headed for the lift, Jodie pushing the pram.

Ten minutes later, Justin was obligingly still sound asleep, parked next to the two women who were relaxing in comfortable seats surrounded by spiky potted greenery. Jodie took a sip of her Cranberry fizz and declared it gorgeous before adding, 'You've no idea how nice it is to be out and in adult company.' Then she helped herself to a French fry.

Aisling smiled. 'Well, I have to say sitting here with you and Justin sipping on a Pink London, and chomping chips is far preferable to bra shopping.' She dunked a fry in sauce and bit into it then fixed her gaze on Jodie. 'C'mon then. Hit me with it. What's it been like?'

Jodie laughed. 'You sure you want to know?'

'The truth, the whole truth and nothing but the truth.'

They'd been chatting for half an hour or so when Justin woke. 'He's going to want feeding,' Jodie said, picking up the warm bundle that was her son. His cries stopped as she began nursing him. She smiled over at Aisling. 'Sometimes, in the middle of the night, when it's just him and me, I feel like I could burst with all the love I feel.'

Aisling felt a deep yearning for her own babies watching Jodie. She was aware, too, that they were being stared at. The handful of patrons who'd bowled in for an after-work drink probably thought them a strange sight. One pregnant woman, one breastfeeding woman and two empty cocktail glasses. She'd have liked to have held up a sign that read, Not that it's any of your business, but they were mocktails!

Jodie looked across the table. She opened her mouth and then closed it again.

'What is it?'

'It's just. Well, I'm pleased we bumped into one another.'

'Me too.'

'To be honest, Aisling, I thought I might have put you off catching up.'

'Why would you think that?'

'Your receptionist probably thought I was a right one the afternoon I called into the guesthouse. I cringe when I think about it. I mean a stranger bursting into tears in front of her like that.' She shook her head. 'I wasn't having a good day with this little man because I'd called in at work to introduce him to my colleagues even though I knew I should have stayed home. He was unsettled and I was overtired.' She gave an ironic little laugh. 'Anyway, I was looking for an ear to bend after I'd put my colleagues yet to start a family off ever having children.

Then I remembered meeting you. The guesthouse was only down the road.'

Aisling was lost. 'I don't understand. You called into O'Mara's?'

Jodie nodded. 'About two weeks ago. I left my number with yer woman on the front desk, but when I didn't hear from you, I just assumed...

'But I never got any message to say you'd called in.' Aisling's mind was racing ahead. 'I'd have called you if I had.'

'Perhaps your receptionist forgot to mention it?' Jodie offered up. 'Either way, I'm glad we caught up this afternoon.'

Aisling gave a weak smile. Bronagh had been back on track after her break over Christmas, or so she'd thought. But the Bronagh she knew and loved would never forget to mention Jodie had been in to see her. It was no use pretending everything was okay because it clearly wasn't. Bronagh was a stalwart of O'Mara's. She was part of the family. Aisling owed it to her to find out what was going on. Her mind made up to broach it first thing in the morning, she focused on Jodie once more and moved the subject on to aqua-jogging.

'That sounds like fun.'

'It is. You should join us.'

'I suppose I could ask my mam if she'd mind Justin for an hour or two.'

'G'won.'

'Aisling O'Mara, you're a bad influence, so you are.' Jodie grinned and helped herself to the last of the chips. 'I will.'

Chapter

Twenty-nine

♥

Aisling had tossed and turned the night before, wondering how to begin the conversation she needed to have with Bronagh without putting O'Mara's longest-standing employee on the defence. She toyed with the idea of talking to Moira or Mammy about how she should play things. Mammy wasn't home, though. She'd gone to line dancing and as she turned to confide in Moira, her sister announced she was knackered and would have an early night. In the end, she'd telephoned Roisin.

She'd moved on from her sulk over none of her family adopting the baby gerbils, and her advice once Aisling had shared her worries was to give it to Bronagh straight. That was easy for her to say when she was in London, she'd thought, thumping her pillow later that night. The jelly beans must have sensed her turmoil too because they'd performed acrobatic stunts into the wee hours. As a result, she felt crumpled and none the wiser, tidying away her breakfast things before heading out of the door of the apartment.

The hoover's steady brmming sounded on the floor below and, being careful to hold on to the banister, Aisling took to the stairs. She felt overbalanced now with her basketball tummy and wondered what it would be like when it reached beach ball size. It was hard to imagine herself lumbering up and down these stairs in the latter stages of her pregnancy, but lumber she'd have to.

She paused on the second-floor landing seeing Ita down the far end pulling the vacuum cleaner about. Jodie had told her the day before the white noise of the machine sent Justin off to sleep and how the house had never been so clean! She wondered if she'd need to resort to daily hoovering with her two jelly beans.

Ita spotted her and waved but didn't stop in her task, intent on reaching the farthest corners of the hallway with the vacuum cleaner nozzle. The old Culture Club hit, 'It's a Miracle' sprang to mind, and Aisling carried on down the stairs humming it. There were no other signs of life until she reached the ground floor and heard the low hum of voices and clattering of knives and forks emanating from below. Instead of her usual routine of going down to the dining room to say good morning to Mrs Flaherty and chat to their guests as they breakfasted, she ventured into reception.

Bronagh was finishing off her Special K and, putting the bowl down, greeted Aisling cheerily before giving her the once-over. 'You look tired, and between you and me, I think it might be time to invest in a new bra.'

Aisling glanced down at her chest. You could always count on Bronagh for honesty. 'I went bra shopping yesterday, only I got sidetracked when I bumped into a woman I met while waiting for my first scan.' She paused and drew breath before rambling on. 'Jodie, her name is, and she had her two-month-old baby boy with her, Justin. He's beautiful, so he is. Anyway, I put the bras I'd picked out back, and we went for a mocktail at the restaurant in Brown Thomas instead. Oh, and these lilies smell gorgeous.' She was waffling, but she couldn't help it and mooching over to the vase on the front desk, she buried her nose in the bouquet. It was a poor attempt to hide her anxiousness. She should have known nothing slipped past, Bronagh, though.

'Since when are you so interested in lilies, Aisling O'Mara?'

'O'Mara-Moran,' Aisling mumbled through the petals.

Bronagh touched her finger to the tip of her nose. 'You've pollen there.'

'I wondered if I could have a word, is all.' Aisling tried to rub the yellow dust off with the back of her hand but succeeded in leaving a yellow smear.

'A word about what?' Bronagh was on high alert now.

'Bronagh, please don't take this the wrong way.' Aisling's eyes were huge as she fixed them on the receptionist.

'For the love of God, Aisling. Would yer spit it out.'

And so she did, glossing over the incidents of forgotten messages and double bookings briefly before telling the receptionist her forgetfulness was worrying her. 'Is caring for your mam and working here too much, Bronagh? Your health must come before any loyalty you feel to O'Mara's.'

'My health?' Bronagh spluttered. 'There's nothing wrong with my health that an injection of oestrogen wouldn't fix, young lady. And why's it taken you so long to talk to me about this? You should have spoken to me as soon as you had any concerns about my work not being up to scratch.'

Bronagh's tone was angry, but Aisling could see the hurt flashing in her eyes. Her insides shrivelled as she tried to formulate a response. 'I'm sorry.' Her voice was small. 'You're right. I should have spoken to you. I've handled this badly, but I convinced myself all you needed was a decent break from this place and that there was no point casting a cloud over your holiday by raising my concerns.' It dawned on Aisling then what had been at the root of her reluctance to talk to Bronagh. 'I was frightened to say anything in case you told me something I didn't want to hear, so I kept putting off talking to you. It's selfish, but Bronagh, you're our rock. I don't know what I, what we'd do without you.' Tears filled Aisling's eyes, turning them bright green, and she reached for the tissues.

'Ah, you silly girl. I'm not going anywhere. C'mere with you.' Bronagh got up from her swivel chair and coming around from the reception desk, she attempted to wrap Aisling in a hug. It was awkward given the size of her girth, but Bronagh was a determined woman. 'I think we need a cup of tea,' she said, releasing Aisling a full minute later.

'With a sugar in mine, please.' Aisling followed Bronagh to the small kitchenette and watched her fill the kettle from the doorway.

Bronagh fetched two mugs and dropped a teabag in each. 'You said there's been double bookings made and messages that haven't been passed on?'

'Yes, and it's been going on for a while now.' Aisling still hadn't got to the bottom of what that was all about.

'Can you remember what specific messages I'm supposed to have forgotten?'

'Well, there was Sara Scott. Remember the hotel inspector?'

'Of course, I remember. We were all on eggshells when yer woman was staying.'

Aisling relayed what had happened and how Freya had come to the rescue. Bronagh didn't look up from her task as she dolloped a spoonful of sugar into Aisling's mug.

'Any others?'

'Other guests have complained, yes.'

'And how long exactly has this been going on?'

Aisling cast her mind back to when things had started to go pear-shaped. 'I suppose about six or so months.'

'I see.'

'And then there's Jodie?' She might as well get it all off her chest, Aisling thought.

'Who's Jodie?'

'The woman I had a mocktail with yesterday. She called in with little Justin to see me, but I wasn't here, so she left her phone number with you to pass on, but I never got it.'

'I don't remember that. When was this?'

'A few weeks ago.' Even as she said it, Aisling realised Jodie had never described Bronagh as the woman she'd spoken to that afternoon. She'd assumed it was Bronagh she was talking about though. Perhaps she'd been too quick jumping the gun.

'I'd remember that, so I would. I'm not dotty. It wasn't me yer woman left a message with, Aisling. Has it occurred to you that all this so-called forgetfulness of mine began when Freya started?'

Aisling stared at Bronagh as she poured the boiling water into the mugs. The blinkers fell away. It made sense, yet at the same time, it didn't because why would Freya lie? What had she hoped to achieve by making Bronagh look like she couldn't do her job? 'You're right,' she said slowly, reflecting on all the occasions Freya had reluctantly, or at least she'd thought she'd been reluctant, told her about Bronagh's slip-ups. 'It did.'

'I had a feeling something wasn't right.' The receptionist's black hair swished as she shook her head.

'Why didn't you say anything?' This time it was Aisling querying Bronagh's reticence in speaking up.

'I thought you had enough on your plate with the babbies.'

Moira too had her doubts where Freya was concerned. God, she'd been so blind. She felt a fool for having the wool pulled over her eyes by the younger woman and guilty for believing what she was telling her without running it past Bronagh. 'I am so sorry, Bronagh.'

Bronagh flapped her hand dismissively. 'We've both been eejits for not saying our piece. There's no point dwelling on it now. We'll have our tea and a custard cream while we ponder what you're going to do about young Miss Freya Lynch. She may be a dishonest madam, but she's also good at her job, and

I don't believe in writing people off without hearing them out properly first. You don't want to cut your nose off to spite your face, Aisling.'

Aisling nodded. The old cliché was true because, under normal circumstances, she'd have had no qualms giving Freya her marching orders, but she was six months pregnant with twins and had been counting on her help.

She took the mug Bronagh was holding out to her, and after a biscuit pit stop, the two women wandered through to the guest lounge to discuss what she should do.

Chapter Thirty

The day dragged, and Aisling ploughed through the entire bag of snowballs she'd successfully hidden from Moira, waiting for four o'clock to roll around. She and Bronagh had decided to speak to Freya together, and at last, the big hand on the clock inched onto twelve and the little hand four. She got up from the table where she'd been unable to settle at her tasks and made her way downstairs.

With each step, Aisling rehearsed what she'd say because it wasn't a conversation she was looking forward to having, but it needed to be had nevertheless.

In her opinion, Bronagh had been generous in her willingness to listen to what Freya had to say for herself. Although Aisling suspected it was for her sake as much as anything. She wondered how her jelly beans were coping with the influx of chocolate and marshmallow and paused to pat her tummy.

Bronagh, who was shuffling papers into a neat pile, looked up and greeted Aisling while Freya, unaware her boss was in reception, called out from where she was hanging her coat up. 'Would you believe I saw blossoms in the Green on my way here today, Bronagh? It's too early, but I suppose it's been mild the last week. I hope the ducks don't all decide to have their ducklings, and then we get hit with a big freeze.' She pulled the kitchenette door to and stepping back into reception smiled at Aisling. 'How're you today, Aisling?'

Aisling tried but found she couldn't summon a smile in return. This young woman had sucked her in with her wide smile. She'd given Freya the benefit of the doubt. Anger simmered at how Freya had made her doubt her trusted staff member, but it wasn't just her she was mad at. Aisling was angry at herself too.

'Is everything alright?' A hint of nervousness made Freya's voice wobble as she clocked the consternation on her employer's face. Her brown eyes flicked to Bronagh, who hadn't shot up from her seat to put on her coat. She couldn't read the older woman's expression, but she could tell that something was amiss.

'Freya, Bronagh and I wanted to talk to you about the mistakes that have been happening at O'Mara's since you started work here. Perhaps we should take a seat in the guests' lounge.' Aisling said.

It wasn't a request.

Freya's face was red as she sat in the chair opposite Aisling and Bronagh, who'd opted for strength in numbers by sitting next to one another on the sofa. A heavy weight had settled in the pit of her stomach because she knew she'd been caught out and she had to fight the urge not to gnaw on her thumbnail. It was a nervous habit she'd tried to break, so she clasped her hands tightly on her lap to distract herself.

There was no beating about the bush as Aisling asked her outright why she'd been dishonest.

Her first instinct was to make out she'd no clue what she was talking about. Her second was to go on the defence. They were ganging up on her. It wasn't fair. Then Freya realised that's what her mam would do. Nothing was ever her mam's fault. Time and time again, she'd seen her pass the buck, worm her way out of things and hadn't she promised herself she'd never be like her? A plump tear rolled down her cheek, but she didn't expect sympathy and knew she didn't deserve any. She was surprised when Bronagh got up, fetched her a tissue, and rested her hand on Freya's shoulder for a brief moment. The small kindness saw her open up.

Her voice was hesitant at first. 'I wanted your job, Bronagh. I saw it as a stepping stone to bigger things. I want to do what you did, Aisling and manage resorts overseas. I suppose I thought I'd get there faster if I could put head receptionist on my resume.' Freya dug deep, determined to be truthful as she examined her actions. 'It's important to me to be in charge.' She shrugged. Maybe it was because of what she'd seen on that holiday to Curracloe, or perhaps it was part of who she was. Whatever made her behave the way she did had to stop, though.

'There's this need, you see, that wells up inside me; no matter what, I have to be the best. I have to be the one who gets patted on the back and praised. It makes me feel in control.' Wasn't the first step to change admitting you needed to change? No matter what happened next, she would learn from it, Freya resolved.

'I loved working here and I'm so sorry, Bronagh, Aisling. I've behaved badly.' She half rose from her seat. 'The worst thing is I've spent my whole life trying not to be like my mam only to find out I'm exactly like her.' Freya was doing her best to hold back the onslaught of tears as, her voice thick, she choked out, 'I'll be on my way then.'

'Sit down, Freya,' Bronagh said, turning to look at Aisling. Her expression told her that she bore no grudge.

Aisling studied her hands for a moment and noticed her fingers were getting plump around her rings. She hoped she wouldn't have to take them off. Her mind played over what Freya had just said, and while she was no psychologist, it was plain to see Freya's behaviour resulted from her upbringing. The apple didn't fall far after all. But that didn't mean she couldn't change. And Freya was wrong about one thing. She wasn't exactly like her mam because from what Aisling had gleaned about Emer Lynch, she knew she wouldn't own her mistakes. Or apologise for that matter. Freya's behaviour was motivated by insecurity and a lack of self-esteem. It didn't make it right, but it helped her understand.

As such, she chose her words carefully.

'Freya, you're good at your job. Very good at it. You don't need to lie to prove that.'

Freya couldn't raise her gaze to meet Aisling's. 'I can see that now, but it was like a compulsion. I couldn't stop myself, and I'm not trying to make excuses; I'm just trying to understand it myself.'

'Bronagh and I don't want you to leave, but you have to promise us both that from here on in, you'll be honest. I believe in second chances, but there won't be a third. Do you understand?'

Freya's nod was emphatic. 'I do, and I promise I won't give you cause for any complaint. Thank you so much, Bronagh, Aisling. You won't regret this.'

Aisling rested her hands on her thighs. She hoped Freya wouldn't let her down, but only time would tell. She was about to heave herself up when Bronagh began speaking.

'Do you know, Freya? I believe we make patterns with our lives. And we don't always get a say. Sometimes the colours in those patterns can be dark and grey. But it's up to us to make sure there's plenty of shiny, bright patches in there too.'

Freya was silent for a moment, thinking of the pattern she was making. The swirling greys had threatened to swallow all the bright patches, but that would change from this moment forth.

Chapter Thirty-one

♥

Three months later

Aisling let Quinn pull the seatbelt across her enormous middle and slot it into place. It was a glorious spring morning, but the beauty of the powder blue sky above them and the burgeoning greenery of the trees as they came back to life after a long winter went straight over her head. She was in no mood for daffodils, baby lambs prancing about, and cotton wool clouds as she rested her head back on the headrest and tried to process what their obstetrician, Dr Keren Kelleher had told them during their appointment.

Bed rest from now until she went into labour.

It was to lower the risk of preterm labour, which was common in multiple birth pregnancies. Aisling had stared at the woman with the voice that could have got her a job reading the evening news on the television as she relayed this information.

Bed rest for what could be another six weeks!

How on earth would she manage it? Panic swelled as she tried to imagine a month of enforced hibernation where the most she had to look forward to in a twenty-four-hour window was meal times and a change of scene each time she went to the loo. It would be different if she didn't feel so good. Enormous, yes, ridiculously so, but full of beans.

'You might feel perfectly healthy, Aisling, but your body is under a lot of stress, and bed rest helps relieve that. Unfortunately, your blood pressure's on the high side too. I'd like to see that come down,' Doctor Kelleher had said.

Quinn had made noises about how it could be worse because some women had to have hospital bed rest for lengthy periods. 'I read about it,' he said. She knew he'd read about it because he liked to share snippets from the book he'd checked out of the library with her now and again. It was akin to when someone suddenly bursts into the chorus of a song on the radio because that's the only line they know. It was annoying. Very annoying, and even though Aisling loved her husband with all her heart right then, she'd have happily told him to feck off. The only thing holding her back was Doctor Kelleher's silken newsreader voice. It was calming so.

Their specialist had interjected that she hadn't ruled hospital bed rest out if Aisling's blood pressure didn't come down. She'd dropped in words like gestational and hypertension as though she was reporting on a global disaster. They were words not to be argued with, and it went without saying the health of her babbies came first. All things considered, she'd had a relatively easy pregnancy, and Quinn was right insomuch that plenty of women in her position didn't have such a straightforward time.

Aisling closed her eyes, opening them as Quinn swore under his breath in time to see a pigeon had decorated the tank's windscreen. She watched the bird poo slide down the glass, thinking it was poetic timing. 'There're tissues in the glove box,' she told him.

He grabbed a handful and clambered out of the car, making it worse as, attempting to clean the poo off, he smeared it across the glass.

Her phone rang, and knowing it would be Mammy wanting a report on their appointment, Aisling sighed. She might as well get the call over and done with.

'Hello, Mammy.' She didn't wait for a response as she got straight to it. 'Dr Kelleher says I'm to have bed rest between now and when I go into labour.'

'She's to have the bed rest, Donal. And are you in bed now, Aisling?'

'No. I'm in the car. Quinn's cleaning bird poo off the wind-screen, and then we'll be heading home.' She wondered if she should talk her husband into making a pit stop at the supermarket for snowballs. She was going to need sustenance.

'She's not in bed yet, Donal. And then you'll be getting into bed as the doctor said?'

'Yes, Mammy.'

'She'll get into bed once she's home, Donal.'

Aisling rolled her eyes but as she heard muffled whispering, a feeling of trepidation stole over her. Mammy was plotting. But what?

'Aisling, Donal and I have discussed it, and we think you and Quinn should come and stay with us here in Howth. You won't have a sea view, not from the guestroom but you'll be very comfortable there. We can even set the spare television up for you. That way, I'll be able to look after you while we wait for the babbies to come.'

'No, Mammy. I want to be at O'Mara's.' It was suddenly imperative to Aisling that she stay where she wouldn't feel cut off from the goings-on of the guesthouse. Bronagh would be able to call up for a cuppa and keep her in the loop, and she'd be on hand should Freya need her. It was familiar. Leila would swing by. Maybe even Jodie would call in. The apartment was home, and that's where she wanted to be. She heard her mammy inhaling, set to argue her point, but headed her off. 'It's very kind of you to offer to have us, Mammy, but Quinn and I will stay at home. And just so you know, Doctor Kelleher said my blood pressure's verging on high, which means I'm not to get worked up.'

'Well, then you'll be wanting to tell your Quinn to tie a knot in it for the foreseeable future.'

'Tie a knot in what?'

'The thing that got you with babbies in the first place.' There was more muffled whispering followed by, 'Well, if Mohammed won't come to the mountain.'

'Mammy, it's if the mountain won't come to Mohammed, and I don't appreciate you calling me a mountain.'

'I was speaking euphorically.'

'Metaphorically, Mammy. And sure, it wouldn't work. We'd all be on top of one another, which wouldn't be good for my blood pressure.'

'Ah, now I've thought of that, so I have. Moira, Tom and Kiera can come and stay at our place for the time being.'

No! Aisling's gaze as the glass cleared and Quinn grinned at her was frantic. 'But, Mammy, Moira will have squatter's rights. Have you thought of that? You might never get her out.'

'Aisling, calm down. I'll be writing a list of house rules, and there'll be no squatter's rights. Now I want you to listen to your mammy. Once you get back to O'Mara's, you're to get into that bed of yours, and as soon as Donal and I get there, I'll bring you some tea and toast. We'll bring the spare television set and set it up in the bedroom for you. I'll make us some nice snacks later, and we can watch Bally K together. It'll be lovely so. Mammy-daughter time.'

Jaysus wept. A slumber party with her mammy, Aisling couldn't wait. 'Mammy, promise me you won't sing the "Soldier-On" song while you're here.'

'Of course I won't sing the song. Sure this is completely different to you trying to get out of doing the cross country running. You've the doctor's permission for one thing.'

'And you are not to make the liver and onions and tell me it's good for the babies.'

There was hesitation.

'Mammy, promise.'

'Alright, Aisling, don't be getting excited now. There'll be no liver and onions on my watch, but I've some lovely kidneys to be frying in the butter for your breakfast. James Joyce himself was partial to the fried kidneys.'

'Well, I'm Aisling O'Mara-Moran, and at the moment, I'm partial to the crisp sandwiches. The green onion flavoured crisp sandwiches in particular.'

Aisling got off the phone then, and as Quinn clambered back into the tank, she broke the news to him.

It was a sombre ride home.

Chapter Thirty-two

♥

One month later

'Right, that's everything.' Quinn zipped up the bag as though they were off on a week's package holiday instead of the hospital. Aisling half expected him to start patting his pockets, looking for his passport. Two brand new white bassinettes, a gift from the Morans, were set up in the room and made up with the sheets Mammy had hot-footed it out to buy. A memory quilt was in pride of place in each crib.

On top of the dresser drawers, folded in neat piles, were the hand knits they'd already received. Bronagh and her mam had been prolific with the cardigans and booties, as had Mrs Flaherty and Mrs Baicu. Rosemary Farrell too had presented her and Quinn with green and yellow booties as promised. Louise, Donal's daughter, had sifted through the baby clothes she'd stored away and presented Aisling with a bag of pristine bibs, hats, and various outfits for both sexes. She'd told her to take anything that wasn't useful to the thrift store. Then there was all Kiera's gear, most of which she'd only been in five minutes before she'd outgrown it.

People had been very generous, and their joy at her and Quinn's joy touched a chord. Right now though, Aisling had something else on her mind because Quinn hadn't packed everything. He'd forgotten something vital.

'Snacks, Quinn. I need snacks. Look, it says so here.' Aisling was sitting on the edge of the bed, barely able to see over her belly. She'd dressed for this momentous occasion in a maternity shirt and the Mo-pants Roisin had sent over a few weeks ago, having sourced a maternity style from the same market she'd frequented for the originals. Maureen had instantly seen an opening for the Mark II version of the Mo-pant and was presently in supply talks with Roisin. Aisling was more concerned with her snacks than Mo-pants; however, she waved the What to Pack for your Hospital Stay checklist she'd had Bronagh print off the internet for her at him.

'I can see that, Aisling, but I don't think snacks means snowballs. Listen, Maureen and Donal are pacing about like caged tigers out there. Why don't I ask them to go to Tescos and pick you up some healthy nibbles?'

'No. Mammy will come back with bags of the scroggin. It's the snowballs I'm needing.' Fear, excitement and anticipation of the caesarean that would be performed in a few hours made Aisling belligerent. She was also hungry because she'd been nil by mouth all morning, allowed only a cup of tea first thing.

'What's this about snowballs?' Roisin appeared in the bedroom doorway waving a bag of chocolate treats.

'Rosi, you're my favourite sister, so you are!' Aisling beamed. 'You will get to hold the babbies first after the grandparents of course.' She'd been so thrilled Roisin and Noah had made the trip across the water not wanting to miss out on the arrival of the twins. There were bonuses to having a pre-planned caesarean, like a definite delivery date.

'Your favourite, you say?' Moira squeezed in alongside her sister with a gift bag. Tom was peering over her shoulder and given the shrieks, Aisling deduced he was holding Kiera. 'Shall I be taking this back then?' Moira waved the bag teasingly.

'What is it?' Aisling asked.

'You'll love it, so you will. Will you call the babbies, Moira and Tom Junior, if I tell you?'

'Feck off, Moira, and give me the bag.'

Moira grinned and handed it to her sister, who produced two travel-size bottles of shampoo and conditioner.

'My Wella Balsam!'

'I can't have any sister of mine with bad hair while they're staying in the hospital, now can I?' Moira grinned.

Aisling knew it was the closest she'd get to an admission of guilt where the use of her salon-only shampoos were concerned from Moira. 'I've two favourite sisters,' she said, correcting her earlier sentiment and you can hold one babby each at the same time.'

'I've got a present for the babies too,' Noah piped up. Nobody was sure where he'd popped up from. 'And Mummy says you're not allowed to say you don't like a present because it's rude. I made this for them.' He thrust a piece of A4 paper at his aunt, which she guessed had come from the printer in reception.

Aisling glanced at Roisin, who shrugged to say it wasn't her idea, but she wasn't buying it.

'Thanks, Noah.' Aisling's eyes scanned what appeared to be an adoption certificate for two gerbils. It was decorated with a coloured picture of what could easily be two rats sitting on top of each other and stick figures which Aisling took to be her Quinn and the babies.

'I did the drawings,' Noah stated proudly.

'They're brilliant, Noah. David Attenborough would be proud, so he would.' Aisling smiled at her nephew and shot daggers at her sister. She'd deal with the adoption formalities after the twins were born.

Maureen was not to be outdone, and she pushed her way into the room, nearly knocking her daughters over. 'I brought you a packet of knickers. There's six of them in there, and they're high waisted, so they are, which means they'll sit above your incision.' She jabbed at her stomach in a cutting motion making everyone in the room wince. 'So you can take those scanty pieces of floss out of that bag, Quinn Moran,' she ordered.

Quinn unzipped the holdall and began to stuff it with the toiletries, snowballs and knickers. He frowned, seeing the adoption certificate and put it to one side. It was enough to get his head around that before this day was done, he'd be a daddy, let alone the adoptive father of babby gerbils.

'Don't do the bag up just yet, Quinn. There's this too.' Donal filled what was left of the space in the room sidling in to pass Quinn a small radio cassette player. He looked at them both. 'There's a tape in there. It's a recording of myself and Mo singing the "Islands in the Stream" song for the babbies in case you need a helping hand settling them while you're in the hospital.'

Maureen and Donal had spent four weeks here at O'Mara's, despite irritations like Donal taking the morning newspaper into the toilet and not reappearing until he'd read it cover to cover and Maureen trying to convince Aisling and Quinn that the pie she'd made for their dinner was steak and onion when it was liver and onion. But, these minor annoyances aside, it had all gone surprisingly smoothly.

Aisling's eyes welled up as she gazed around at her family squished into the room. 'Thanks a million all of yer. For everything.'

'I think it's time we got this show on the road,' Quinn said, zipping up the bag once more before slinging it over his shoulder.

'I'll take that downstairs for you,' Donal said.

Quinn sized his wife up. It would be a two-man job to get down the stairs. 'Tom, would you mind giving Aisling and me a hand.'

'You could start by helping me up.' Aisling held her hand towards him.

'Watch your back, Tom,' Moira bossed, sounding like her mammy's daughter. 'Bend your knees. You're only after getting over the calf strain.' Tom and Quinn had been taking their marathon training seriously.

'Aisling, are you sure I can't—'

Aisling cut Maureen off. 'No, Mammy. I've told you there's only one person allowed in the delivery room with me, and that's Quinn.'

'Will they have a window where I can stand to watch them be born like.'

'Jaysus wept, Mammy. There's no window. It's an operating theatre.'

'On the count of three, Aisling,' Tom said, grasping her hand.

Quinn pulled the tank over before Tom helped Aisling into the car and Donal put her bag on the back seat. Bronagh had abandoned her post to come and stand alongside Maureen, Roisin, Moira and Noah and as Tom closed the car door and Quinn parped the horn, they began to wave and blow kisses. The tank pulled away from the kerb and Aisling turned her neck, determined to wave until she couldn't see them anymore, and it was then she saw the rainbows.

'Quinn, there's a rainbow over O'Mara's.'

'Two of them, Quinn said, grinning. And then it was time to go and meet their babbies.

O'Mara-Moran – Quinn and Aisling are proud to announce the arrival of their son Connor Finley and daughter Aoife Lily born at 11.55 and 11.58 pm on June 5, 2002. The third and fourth grandchildren for Maureen O'Mara and the fifth and sixth grandchildren for Donal McCarthy. The first grand-children for Maeve and Cathal Moran. Much loved by their cousins Noah and Kiera, all their aunties and uncles and lots of new friends. Watched over now and forever by their grand-father and Maureen's beloved, late husband, Brian O'Mara.

The End

Thanks so much for reading Rainbows over O'Mara's. If you enjoyed this latest instalment in the O'Mara family's lives please recommend the books to other readers and leave a review or starred rating on Amazon or Goodreads. I'd so ap-preciate it!

There are more O'Mara family shenanigans coming soon in...

An O'Mara's Reunion – Book 13, The Guesthouse on the Green series. Out 18 December 2022 - Pre-order here: http s://books2read.com/u/bo2A8v

Also if you enjoy the O'Mara family stories then I have a new series introducing, the Kelly family from Emerald Bay on Ireland's wild west coast. Book 1, Christmas in the Little Irish Village is out on October 14   https://geni.us/B0BBNGK43Bc over

Welcome to the little Irish village where Christmas celebrations are in full swing! Twinkling lights, cosy fires and big mugs of hot chocolate are in abundance as Shannon Kelly returns home to the Shamrock Inn. Will this be the year she finds the man of her dreams or is she

destined to be forever unlucky in love?

Thirty-four-year-old Shannon is heartbroken following an unexpected break up. Seasonal joy is the last thing on her mind, as she wonders if she'll ever find the kind of long-lasting love she's always dreamed of. Even the comforting distractions of her big Irish family can't cheer her up. Then things get even worse when Shannon slips over on the ice and finds herself red-faced in the arms of a gorgeous American man...

Despite the embarrassing encounter, Shannon can't help wondering who the handsome stranger is. She soon finds out when **James Cabot** takes a room at the Shamrock Inn. Their second meeting is equally disastrous when she gives James the tour – without realising her skirt is tucked into her knickers! Shannon isn't sure how she's going to survive living under the same roof when she has such a talent for making a complete eejit of herself, and resolves to avoid their new guest at all costs.

But when Shannon discovers James is in Ireland because he's claiming to be the long-lost grandson of her elderly neighbour, Maeve Doolin, she is immediately suspicious. Shannon has known kind Maeve since she was a little girl and feels protective of her, so she's determined to find out the truth. Even if it means spending more time with James...

The two of them end up getting closer than she'd bargained for when they take a tour of Emerald Bay and end up snowed in together. But just as James begins to make Shannon's heart melt with his cheeky grin and awful carol singing, a shocking secret threatens to shatter the growing romance between them.

Can Shannon trust James? And will she get the happi-

ly-ever-after she's been hoping for this Christmas?

This gorgeous festive romance is the perfect cosy read to snuggle up with this Christmas. Fans of Nicola May, Trisha Ashley and Debbie Macomber will love this wonderfully uplifting novel.

https://geni.us/B0BBNGK43Bcover

About Author

Michelle Vernal lives in Christchurch, New Zealand with her husband, two teenage sons and attention seeking tabby cats, Humphrey and Savannah. Before she started writing novels, she had a variety of jobs:

Pharmacy shop assistant, girl who sold dried up chips and sausages at a hot food stand in a British pub, girl who sold nuts (for 2 hours) on a British market stall, receptionist, P.A...Her favourite job though is the one she has now – writing stories she hopes leave her readers with a satisfied smile on their face.

Visit Michelle at www.michellevernalbooks.com to find out more about her books, and when you subscribe to her monthly newsletter, you'll receive a free O'Mara family short story to say thank you.

Facebook: https://www.facebook.com/michellevernalnovelist

Also by, Michelle Vernal

Book 13 – An O'Mara's Reunion 18 December, 2022,
Pre-order here: https://books2read.com/u/bo2A8v
Liverpool Brides Series
The Autumn Posy
The Winter Posy
The Spring Posy
The Summer Posy
Isabel's Story
The Promise
The Letter

And new fiction coming October 14
Christmas in the Little Irish Village

Printed in Great Britain
by Amazon

39700742R00128